PARENTS' DAY

A N

EDWARD CANDY

LONDON
VICTOR GOLLANCZ LTD
1967

MADE AND PRINTED IN GREAT BRITAIN BY
THE GARDEN CITY PRESS LIMITED
LETCHWORTH, HERTFORDSHIRE

FOR
ISABEL WINTHROPE

AUTHOR'S NOTE

The line quoted on page 118 is from Eric Crozier's libretto for Benjamin Britten's "Little Sweep" *(Let's Make an Opera)*.

I

ALL SUMMER LONG, and it would be a long sweet summer, Owen Pinnegar had been haunted by a fear not irrational enough to dismiss; to write off, say, as one of the symptoms of his illness. On the Saturday of the Whitsun holiday crowded roads, crowded restaurants, pavements so crowded even in a country town as to be impassable had given to his apprehensions a solid form. He could not laugh off what he had read in his Sunday paper—that by the end of the century the population of this planet would have doubled, or trebled, or multiplied a thousandfold, he could not quite remember which: he did not expect, especially after the events of the last few weeks, that he should witness this phenomenon in his own flesh, but his sons and daughters would doubtless be affected by it, and he was a man whose children's future health and happiness counted above all gratifications of his own. In the same newspaper a figure had been given, at least he thought it had been given, implying that each member of the human race should then have only twenty square feet of earth to call his own; barely enough for his daughter Tess to show off a skirt in, or his son Jude to stretch full length in lazy grace of sunlight, should sunlight penetrate the miasma of so packed a populace. In his wiser moments Owen knew that this figure could not be right. Would not the Sahara have been reclaimed? Might not emigration to other planets be a commonplace? But Owen's wiser moments did not last very long, and in the crumpled mornings when he hardly knew whether to sleep again and risk a nightmare or to lie awake and deliberately create one he was haunted by a constant absurd vision, constant in the threat of the whole, though varying as to detail: a field, perhaps, a long stretch of seashore, a forest of tall trees, any or all of these so filled with people that only by the most tender self-effacement could he pass this way or that without the recurrent brutality of contact. His facial expression was generally thought, even now, to be apologetic : what new diffidence might it not achieve when the tact that ordered his conduct in all important matters should be called into play with every step he took?

"Naturally the roads were bad at Whitsun," his wife said one evening in early July. "They cannot surely be so bad tomorrow?" He would have liked, from any angle, to agree with her. Support of this kind generally passed between them almost as often as words and glances : but her real doubt, the doubt underlying the certainty of the clear positive lying look she gave him, raising her eyes from the pullover she was knitting for their younger son, was not to be turned off lightly. The roads, he thought, could be as bad or worse than they had been at Whitsun.

"Of course," she now said, threading her needle with a slight frown, "we could go by train if you are really worried about the traffic."

"How could we? From Cardigan or Carmarthen we should have to get a bus to Newcastle Emlyn and from there a taxi to Cilrheddyn. Goodness knows what the bus services are like or what a taxi would cost. And the last train back from Cardigan leaves so early : we would miss the concert and the children would be disappointed."

"You looked up the trains then?" Helen said with a little air of triumph.

"Well, naturally. It was only sensible to look : I would far rather go by train if it were possible. But it isn't, so we had better forget about it."

"It is a great pity that I don't drive," Helen said. It was possible to detect a faint reproach in her words, and Owen was capable of detecting reproach anywhere. But in fact her not learning to drive was as much by her wish as his own : traffic frightened her, and while she could keep to herself what she suffered in the passenger seat she rather thought that overmuch imagination was a handicap behind the wheel. Until recently Owen had seen no point in his wife's being able to handle a car, since there was no chance of their ever possessing more than one; but now he just wondered if she were wondering how she should manage in the years ahead with three of their four children so far away and travel by train so impossibly dear.

"You could have lessons between now and the end of term," Owen said, taking a cat upon his knee and stroking it. "There, poor puss, you will be all on your own tomorrow. I hope you won't be lonely."

"It is the birds you should be sorry for," Helen said, fastening off her thread. She held her work out for Owen to admire.

"Yes, it is very nice. But isn't it far too big? Surely Jude could wear that, and I thought you were knitting it for Diggory."

"Diggory likes them to come down to his knees," his wife said simply, "and I always leave some room for growth. And all their pullovers shrink in the school laundry. Perhaps they boil them, or don't rinse them properly. So if I make them three sizes too big at the start . . ."

Her voice trailed off; she leaned forward and slapped at Owen's knee.

"A flea! Owen, the cat has fleas again!"

"She is never without them," Owen said, and put the cat on the ground, for they were sitting on deckchairs outside the french windows of their drawing room. She did not give him a backward glance but walked stiffly towards the nearest flowerbed, her tail vertical with disdain.

"I hope you haven't been bitten?" Helen said in a little wail. "Bites keeping you awake tonight of all nights!"

"She was only on my lap for a few minutes," Owen said, "and I have some of that cream the doctor gave us for Tamsin after she sat on the ant-heap."

Helen's anxieties were at rest: she folded the pullover.

"I will take this in and iron it. What is the time, Owen? Tamsin should be home, I want her to go to bed in good time."

"It is barely eight."

Helen went inside and Owen listened for his daughter's voice in the neighbour's gardens or outside in the quiet suburban street. Beyond the garden fence one of these neighbours mowed his grass; the lawn was small, the mower large, the length of time taken by the operation seemed out of all proportion and Owen wondered whether Mr. Thompson, who did not look romantic, simply went round and round his patch of grass for the sheer joy of propelling a powerful machine. "Can it be that I am envious?" Owen asked himself as he got up and went to the shed to bring out his own hand mower; but Helen called through the kitchen window in a voice that contrived to be both sharp and tender, "Dear, do you think you should? Leave it until

9

Sunday and I will do it." Owen closed the shed door and listened to the sound of his heart beating. He had got up from his chair, he thought, rather quickly, and Helen's words had awakened his dormant fears; fear had the power to hasten a heartbeat. Surely not for so long, though? Surely within a few moments a healthy heart would receive calming messages from the brain and subside into a gentler rhythm? He thought of going back to his deckchair, but the cat had seized her chance and occupied it; he did not like to turn her off. He went into the house, passing Helen in the kitchen. Her quick glance discerned something of what he felt; in the greyness of his spare features she saw enough to withdraw the colour from her own cheeks. Words came to her lips but she did not utter them: unuttered they might annul the situation that called them forth. She went on with her ironing, listening to his tread on the stairs. His step was as slow as an old man's.

Into their suspended quiet, supplanting those pleas and intimations that passed wordlessly between them, the ring of the telephone stridently broke. Owen paused and turned, Helen reached the hall before him. He saw the change in her expression from gravity to delight; even without hearing her greeting he knew it must be one of their older children.

"Yes, Daddy is here, dear. Owen, Tess wants to speak to you. He is just coming, Tess. How are you, dear, how is Jude, there is nothing wrong, is there? And Diggory, is Diggory all right?"

She held the telephone out to her husband accepting her daughter's impatient, "No, no, there is nothing wrong with any of us!" completely and at once. Tess was truthful, and not yet given to sparing her mother; Tess's word could be taken and visions of broken legs, polio, snakebite dismissed. Helen's brow cleared as Owen's clouded.

"Say it all again, dear, and slower this time. I could hardly follow you."

Tess said it all again, slowly and clearly as if she were speaking to an idiot child and at a high enough pitch for Helen to hear all that Owen heard.

"Oh, no. No, I am sorry, Tess, I hate to disappoint you, but that is really impossible. I am touched, I am very pleased that you thought of me, but how can I possibly do such a thing?"

Helen fiercely nodded: even if she had not heard her daughter's request she would have resisted it. Any activity beyond the common run was out of Owen's range for the moment: the common run was, God knows, strain enough.

"Yes, I know it, I know it well; I have played parts of it with Jude. Last holidays I went through the first movement with him. But there is a difference—my dear, you must see what a difference there is!"

"Let me speak to her," Helen said and made a movement to take the telephone from him. This he resisted.

"Just a moment, Tess. It is all right, Helen, I would not think of doing it, there is no need to worry. Tess, I told your mother there is no need for her to worry, I have no intention of making a fool of myself in public. How would you feel, listening to my mistakes!"

"I have listened to Daniel's mistakes for weeks," his daughter said, over a hundred miles away. He could see the tears in her brilliant eyes as clearly as if she stood beside him. "Honestly, Daddy, you couldn't be any worse. Daniel was terrible, he nearly drove Jude mad. Please, please try."

"I haven't even got the music!" Owen cried in despair.

"Let me speak to her," Helen said, and this time took the telephone. "Now, Tess dear, it is all very sad if you cannot do as you planned, and we were looking forward to it as well, so we know how disappointed you must be."

"It is Jude," her daughter moaned. "It was to be the last thing, you see, his farewell performance. Everyone was looking forward to it for his sake."

"Perhaps he could play something else?" Helen said, but her tone wavered: her daughter had unerringly found the weak spot in her defences, for only her son's pain could ever touch her more deeply than her husband's.

"Of course he could, but it wouldn't be the same. You don't begin to understand what this means to him."

"Is he there? Can I speak to Jude? I could explain why it is out of the question."

"No, no," Owen said quickly: and, putting his hand over the mouthpiece of the telephone. "You know that we agreed to say nothing to them before the end of term."

Helen's eyes opened very wide; then she said in a cool, distinct voice, never looking away from Owen's face, "Daddy hasn't the music, dear. And there is no time for him to practise."

"The score is in the Public Library," Tess said with inexorable calmness. "And if you get here by eleven they could practise together before and after lunch. Jude is sure," she said, descending to pathos, to flattery, "Daddy could manage the larghetto, and he would help him with the variations. And it's a whole term's work wasted if we don't play it. Tim will be sick too; he has slaved over his part."

"I believe I could manage it, Helen," Owen said, scarcely above a whisper. "You can hear how upset she is. You can guess how Jude must feel."

She could indeed guess. Jude's talent as a clarinet player, suspected while his hands were still too small and his chest too weak for him to do it justice, had swelled with his physical frame, and was now established on a sounder basis than mere parental pride or the hopes of his teachers. A visiting woodwind player of international repute had offered to take him as his pupil at the end of the summer. In the midst of personal terror Owen had found some solace in the possibility of his boy's bright future : Helen had folded away this splendid joy with a good housewife's intention of storing it against a season of need. "I will go to the library," she said now. "If the score is there we will see what can be done. But tell Jude Daddy makes no promises. He will have to think about it."

"Can I speak to him? I knew you would do it," Tess said to her father. "I told Jude so."

"And what did he say?" Owen asked drily.

"Well, he rather thought you wouldn't," Tess said. "He thought you would think you weren't good enough."

"Tell him beggars can't be choosers."

"I did," Tess said, and Helen wondered at Owen's rueful smile. "So he is used to the idea. He will go through the variations with Tim tonight to see which bits you are likely to find difficult."

"Thank him for me," Owen said in his mild voice. "You must ring off now, dear, while you still have some pocket money left. We will see you tomorrow."

"All right. Make it early. See you."

She hung up.

"What is wrong with Daniel Hardy?" Helen said, "because if it is just that he doesn't play very well they might have decided to drop him weeks ago. There are plenty of other young violinists, they have never been short of string players."

"Nobody has dropped Daniel," Owen said. "Tess was not very clear, but I think she said that Daniel had refused to play and gone off in a huff."

"Poor Daniel! If he would not play to please Tess he must have been finding it a burden indeed."

"You don't suppose, Helen," her husband now said with a little awkwardness, "that there is any need to take this thing between Tess and Daniel seriously? Because I would not like to think she was in love with a moody, strange, unreliable boy."

"Boys who are not those things at seventeen or eighteen would be hard to find," Helen said with her appeasing smile, "and Tess is just the sort of girl to pick a lame dog. She has your soft heart."

He still looked thoughtful; he did not like to think of his girl devoting herself to a succession of prickly youths.

"There is Tamsin now," Helen said. "Will you give her her milk and the sandwiches I made her whilst I go to the library?"

Owen roused himself and went to let his younger daughter in. Helen combed her hair and powdered her nose, slipped a light coat over her light dress and went out with a kiss for Tamsin on the way. Owen saw her walking down the road as he put Tamsin's meal on the kitchen table; her step had more spring in it, her head was held higher than he had seen it for weeks past. "She thinks that this will take my mind off my condition," he said to himself with tender amusement. "She would rather I took things easy as the doctors say I should, but since I can help Jude by a little exertion that risk must be balanced against my morbid and unceasing preoccupation with my illness. It is your soft heart that Tess has inherited, Helen."

"Where has Mummy gone?" Tamsin reasonably demanded.

"To the library, to get me some music. Tess rang up. She and Jude are playing tomorrow and Daniel Hardy was to have played as well and now can't, or won't. So I am to take his place. I am to play the first violin part in the Mozart Clarinet Quintet."

He spoke out loud and in wonder at what he had undertaken

13

to do, not for the little girl's benefit. Nothing surprised Tamsin much. She assumed from the happy vantage point of her nine years that Jude was to be famous all the world over, that Tess would be as fine a viola player as he was a clarinettist, that her father was as splendid a musician as either. She also knew that her mother baked the best cakes and knitted the best pullovers in the world; only in relation to Diggory, the nearest to her in the family in age and accomplishments, did she attach the slightest sense of the conditional. She rather thought that two more years' piano practice than she herself had yet had ought to have made Diggory strike fewer wrong notes; she often told him so in the holidays, and he replied that not all of a family could be musical. "Tess is not much good really," he once remarked, "but at a small school like Cilrheddyn she does well enough." His arrogant tone provoked Tamsin to physical retaliation on behalf of Tess, Cilrheddyn, womanhood in general, small schools the country over. "At a school like Dad's," he had maddeningly continued, "Tess wouldn't get a chance to play at a Parents' Day concert."

"Daddy's school doesn't have Parents' Days," Tamsin said, "and even if hundreds of them play the viola what's the good of that? They don't have concerts because they're all so busy working for examinations."

"You are only repeating what you have heard Mum say," Diggory said with demonstrable patience. "And it is no use despising examinations, my girl. You will never be able to earn your own living without paper qualifications."

"I don't despise examinations, I do jolly well in them," Tamsin said, "and so does Tess, and Jude would too if he didn't spend so much time practising."

She could have bitten out her tongue, but Diggory did not pounce on her at all. Instead he said quite kindly,

"It is different for Jude. He will make his living that way. Of course he will never be rich, but he probably doesn't think riches matter."

"You are sure to be rich, Diggory, you are so good at thinking of ways to make money."

"I am not musical," Diggory said dispassionately, "so it seems only fair that I should have some special talent of my own. And when Jude falls on hard days and Tess is sick of playing her fiddle in the gutter for pennies I daresay you will all be glad of my practical turn of mind."

"Daddy will look after us," Tamsin said at once.

"Poor little Tamsin," Diggory said. "Our father will not live for ever. And he has spent so much on our education that he will leave his widow and orphans penniless."

"He won't have to spend any more on Jude, Jude has a scholarship. And Tess is paid for by the corporation because of her asthma. So it is only you and me."

"You and I will cost a thousand pounds a year, and that is almost half Dad's salary."

"How do you know?"

"Jude told me. And Jude said it is lucky for us Daddy decided not to grow his hair and play the violin in an orchestra or he wouldn't have been able to feed us all, let alone send us to Cilrheddyn."

"Then Jude won't be able to have any children?"

"Jude will live from hand to mouth," Diggory said with relish. "I shall give him something very nice each year at Christmas. That will be kind of me, and it will teach Jude to be thankful that I haven't got perfect pitch or a good sense of rhythm or any of those things."

Then he had gone off to practise for half an hour and Tamsin thought he had made more mistakes than ever, in a rather triumphant way.

"Did you want another sandwich?" Owen said, coming back into the room with his violin in its case.

"No. I'll get myself a banana. Have I got to have a bath?"

"Mummy didn't say."

"Then I won't. Are there violins in a clarinet quintet? I thought there would be five clarinets."

"There is one clarinet, that is Jude. Then two violins, Ian Donald and me. A viola, Tess. And Tim Murdoch will play the 'cello."

"Can I learn the 'cello at Cilrheddyn?"

"Perhaps. It will depend on if we could buy one secondhand. They cost a lot of money."

"If I save my pocket money for two and a half years, would that be enough?"

"Not nearly. But it would help," he added quickly, seeing her face fall. "Tamsin, you must not count too much on going to Cilrheddyn. We might not be able to afford it."

He had spoken not quite without thinking, but without thinking quite enough. When Tess had gone away in tears and terror, vouched for by her doctor and paid for by the ratepayers, he and Helen had spent months in devising ways of sending Jude after her. To promise her Jude in a year's time was not to sacrifice Jude, they had long known that none of the local schools would look with a kind eye on his single-minded pursuit of a different goal from most : and for Tess the prospect of leaving home was made more bearable by the knowledge that the school would be small, that there would be boys as well as girls. "That is how schools should be," Owen said after their first visit : and thought with bitterness of the school in which he worked, and where he was to become second master. This school had fine buildings, fine grounds, fine equipment, some fine teachers, all men. Detecting a note of apology in his own voice when a colleague asked him if his son had inherited his mathematical ability, detecting pity in that colleague's face when he replied, no, Jude showed no particular interest in anything but music, Owen made up his mind, and Jude followed Tess. His fees made a great hole in the Pinnegars' income, and Diggory's neatly took away all the increments and concessions the next five years added to Owen's salary. Tamsin could only follow Diggory if Helen went back to work, and she was ready and eager to do this, was already attending shorthand and typing classes to get her speeds up to standard. "And just as well, too," Owen told himself not infrequently in these days, "for she will be able to keep herself and Tamsin at home, and the others' school fees are insured. But of course Tamsin will not be able to go to Cilrheddyn, and we had better let her just gently and gradually know that she must not take it for granted."

But a revelation is never gradual, though it may be gently made. On this summer evening a little doubt about a new hope— for the 'cello was no more than that—had been lost in a tremendous doubt about an old certainty. For nearly seven years this child had been driven back and forth to see Tess, then Tess and Jude, now Tess, Jude, and Diggory. She knew the journey by heart, the wooded, watered Pembrokeshire landscape, the little town just over the border into Cardiganshire where they took the older children to lunch, the river a few miles away at Cenarth, the warm sea at Tresaith. She knew her brothers' friends, the school, its garden and grounds, the corner where rabbits and guinea pigs were kept, the shabby hall where the yearly concerts were held as the climax of Parents' Day. She was a child deeply attached to her home, and there were times when she wondered if she could ever sleep without her mother's goodnight kiss or live through a week without her father's daily concern for her content : but Jude and Tess and Diggory lived, and she supposed that she would too. To be told now that this mild degree of heroism might never be asked of her, and the attendant reward of all she looked forward to snatched away without, it seemed, any reference to those fears and hopes, was too much, it was too sudden, she was overwhelmed. Relief and despair flooded her heart at the same moment; she could not disentangle them, she wept. When Helen came in with Owen's score she was in bed, still weeping, and Owen was standing by her bedroom window with a face of stone.

II

W H E N T E S S C A M E out of the telephone kiosk a big young man of loosely hearty appearance detached himself from a shop window nearby and walked over to meet her. This was Tim Murdoch, who taught her music; that is to say he sat beside her twice a week while her fairly skilful fingers dealt in a businesslike way with the exercises and pieces she selected for herself and assured him he would find proper for her. He played 'cello and viola himself, fairly well, just enough better than Tess to criticise her occasionally when his courage was high. The violin he loved but played poorly. He was happier on the piano, happiest of all talking, and he could talk with knowledge and vivacity on any subject that touched his own. He was Tess's senior by less than six years, and the gap in their ages seemed to close day by day.

"Any luck?" he said, knowing the answer. Tess dejected was Tess immobile; her quick step and the swing of her long straight hair showed Tess triumphant.

"Oh, Dad will do it. I knew he would."

"You knew nothing of the kind. You said he might and looked doubtful."

"Well, he is modest. He is not a bit like Jude. But he is ever so good, Tim, truly. He would have been a professional but he met Mummy when he was in the army and they got married and he could get a better grant if he went in for teaching, so he did. He was good at maths, too, like Diggory. Jude and I don't seem to have inherited that."

"How greedy you are, Tess Pinnegar. Diggory doesn't begrudge you your powers."

"No, he thinks so little of them. My mother says Diggory will keep his head whatever happens. Do you think we could have some fish and chips while we are down here, Tim?"

"If you have any money. I am penniless till the end of the month."

Tess looked in her purse.

"I have enough for one bit of fish and not very many chips. Or we could have a lot of chips and eat them out of newspaper. But they don't like you to hang about the shop with only chips. I wish I had brought some more money; then there would be enough fish for both of us and we could have a table and tomato sauce."

Tim looked at her in wonder; her greed, coupled with her narrow body, never ceased to astound him. Tess seldom if ever stopped eating to his knowledge. Before starting on a tricky bit of bowing she would unwrap a toffee and push it into her cheek : only then could she concentrate. "It is because I was on a diet for years," she once said, when he suggested her teeth might suffer from this treatment even if her shape did not. "First I had eczema, then I had asthma, I expect I shall start having migraine soon, so I mean to enjoy my food before somebody puts me on another diet. Next time it might be no chips, no chocolate. Think of that!"

He did think : he fixed his mind on it while they went into the fish and chip shop. She finally settled for two steak pies, cheaper than fish, and not very many chips after all. He put most of his on her plate and they sat side by side at a table in the window.

"Supposing Daniel changes his mind tomorrow morning," Tess now said, "wouldn't I feel a perfect fool?"

"I told you we should have asked Matthew before we rang your father," he said, naming their headmaster.

"We looked for Matthew, didn't we? I would have asked, if I could have. Tomato sauce?"

"No, thank you," he said with restraint and looked away while she shook the bottle over her food with a free hand. "Don't take too long, Tess. We shall have to find the Old Man when we get back."

"You know what he's like the day before Parents' Day. Wouldn't it be better not to bother him now we know Daddy will take Daniel's place?"

"He must be told. He particularly wanted Daniel to play." Tim stopped abruptly, aware of a difficulty : Tess was not looking at him, but she looked up now.

"Matthew wanted Daniel to play, why on earth?" Tim did

not answer this question, which was actually less a question than a comment on Matthew, whom Tess considered eccentric to the point of lunacy; and on Daniel of whose capacity to play any instrument with skill she had the most vivid doubts, and this in spite of liking Daniel at least as much as she liked Tim. Tim did not answer because he felt he had betrayed a confidence; he was thankful when she went back to her food, evidently attempting to puzzle out this new idea for herself. They finished their meal in silence, they went out in silence to his Lambretta, she climbed on to the pillion and they shot away out of the town and up the hill towards the school, four miles off. It was an evening of calm beauty, they sang, though the light wind took away their song and their breath together. "Pom pom, pom pom, tiddle-iddle pom pom," Tim shouted over his shoulder. "Will your father be able to manage the variations, do you think? Some of them are bloody difficult, I can tell you."

"My father can do anything," pink Tess shouted back with glowing eyes and cheeks faintly greasy but as yet unspotted. "Wait until you hear him! Pom pom, pom pom, tiddle-iddle pom pom! Oh, I can't wait for tomorrow!"

The road bent sharply, launched itself full tilt at the Cych river, turned again only just in time and ran alongside the little dark stream under a profusion of tall trees, young oaks and birch; long fine shadows barred the road almost into darkness but high overhead the sky sparkled and shone through leaf after flickering leaf. A mile from Cilrheddyn the road took another prodigious turn and climbed a hundred feet out of the valley; at the next bend there was a post box and a concrete platform where churns of milk were left to be taken to Cardigan, Carmarthen, St. Clair. Just now the churns had company; a small neat young woman with colourless hair blessed with a look of gold by the late light and a face the very reverse of Tess Pinnegar's, a face made for secrets, for hints and reservations. Tess saw this person without enthusiasm, but Tim drew up with a greeting altogether too ardent for his passenger's taste. She could see nothing very delightful in a chance encounter with Celia Spurgeon, who taught her French and was supposed by all the children to be in love with Tim. Tim and Celia knew that she was not; but even if she could have put an end to the talk she would not have done so. In the silly whispers her real thoughts and feelings escaped comment; and since she was ashamed of the direction those thoughts and feelings sometimes took she smiled and looked down when her name was linked with Tim's.

"This is where I get off and walk," Tess said with a certain grimness.

"Would you very much mind, Tess? I promised to be back before half past eight to help Janet do the flowers."

"You have cut it very fine," Tess said, with a glance at her watch. "If we hadn't come along you couldn't have got there in time."

"Yes," Celia said in the meek voice Tess despised. "I should have left my letter for the morning post."

"Or asked me to take it for you," Tim said, betraying a confidence for the second time in less than an hour, "since you knew I would be going."

"I shall enjoy the walk," Tess said, with a heightened colour at this evidence of collusion; and she set off at once, not wishing to be delayed by the polite things Celia would say or the kind ones Tim was preparing. "How could he tell her?" she asked herself, striding downhill, for the road had abandoned its climb as hopeless and was rushing back to the safe proximity of the river. "What has she to do with the concert, with Daniel's desertion and my idea, that I meant nobody but Tim to know until I was sure that it would work!" Then she thought that none of these things would in the least interest Celia, for whom music was, as she was fond of saying, a closed book : but that Tim's advent on the lovely, lonely road might interest her very much, enough to send her out to meet them in spite of her arrangement with Janet. "And she will be late for Janet," Tess cried in chagrin, "she will, because they are still up there at the top of the hill, I can't hear Tim's engine starting up, they are just talking as if Janet and Matthew were of no importance at all."

She began almost to run, but had to give it up, for the road now deteriorated, its surface cracked and crumbled, a ridge of delicate grass ran along the middle. On her right the river inconsequently turned away, then back, then settled for the other side of the road; on the stone bridge that spanned it her brother Jude was sitting, throwing loose stones from the parapet into the water. Each separate splash sounded a moment like a plucked string above the constant murmur of the current; he saw his sister, actually he saw her before she saw him, but gave no sign. As she came nearer she saw that his face was full of a complex disturbance; her divergent feelings, exaltation over the success with her father, anger at Celia's annexation of the young man she, Tess, was almost ready to love, gave way to another sensation, much more familiar, that of anxious care for Jude, who wanted nothing of the kind.

"What is it, Jude? If it is Daniel you needn't worry, it is all settled. Tim and I have settled everything."

"What have you settled?" the boy said, not looking up from the river, nor altering by a jot the troubled arrangement of his features.

"I telephoned home, I spoke to both of them, and Daddy will do it. Aren't you glad?"

She faltered over the question, it was so unnecessary. Nothing in his look suggested gladness. She did not know what that look did suggest.

"You knew I would ask him, we talked of it."

"I thought it was a joke," he said morosely, and turned away from her. A larger stone plopped into the river, a fountain of little drops rose to sprinkle his angry face.

"You did not, Jude, you were as serious about it as I was, or Tim. And I arranged it for you, for you! What do you think I care whether we play the quintet or not? I could play my chaconne or the sonata, it means nothing to me."

She was bristling with wounded pride, another word and she would be in tears. Jude supplied the other word.

"Then if I don't care to play, why should you worry?"

She gathered herself together and launched herself, tears and all, at what she thought his tenderest point.

"I should like to see the day when you don't care to play, Jude Pinnegar! You love it, the clapping and the oo-s and the ah-s and everyone smiling up at you as if you were a pop singer or something!"

"That isn't what I love," Jude said, with a gravity that made her to her own sense irrelevant, abysmal. Then he added, scrupulously enough. "I don't say I don't like it, but it never goes on for long enough."

"Nothing would ever go on long enough for you," Tess flung out, and turned her back on him. Over her shoulder she threw off, "You'd better get back to school. Tim's going through the last movement with you, in case you've forgotten."

She did not wait for him, her fury gave her the impetus to cover the remaining quarter of a mile at some speed. Tim and Celia on the scooter overtook her with a wave as she turned into the drive; Tess did not wave back, she pretended not to have seen them. She did however see, out of the corner of her eye, Jude's shambling, sagging, dejected figure plodding with a certain weariness in their wake. Her wrath abated : she felt a warm conviction that he would now be reasonable. Whatever had upset him earlier would vanish with her own sharp words as soon as he joined Tim in the music room. She forebore to wave to him, in case he treated her with the same coldness she had just shown Celia Spurgeon. Such coldness from Jude would kill her.

"Well, I am here," Celia was to say some ten minutes later in a light way that seemed to deny any need for an apology at her failed appointment, at the same time that her placatory look offered one.

"So you are," Janet Storace said quite amiably. She was in the kitchen, which was cool and almost dark at this hour. The evening meal had been served and cleared away before seven, the Spaniards, all four of them, had driven into Newcastle Emlyn in José's old Morris. "Make sure you are back in good time," Janet had said, coming into the kitchen with buckets full of flowers she had picked before breakfast and left all day in the cellar, "tomorrow will be a busy day for all of us." José promised an early return with solemnity, but she put as little faith in his promises as in Celia Spurgeon's. "You do too much," her brother Matthew sometimes told her. "If you would just not do everyone else's work for them they would turn to and do it themselves."

"Or they would leave," Janet said, revealing her estimate of what she did for her brother's school. As it was exactly the same as his own they could not really quarrel about the weight she carried, with on the whole such good grace, such ready forbearance, for the children as well as her brother, for Celia as well as the Spaniards.

"Meg has been helping me," she now said, her hands busy

with fronds of a small leaved fern that grew exuberantly in the hedgerows. "Now she can get back to her own work."

"I have no talent for this sort of thing," Meg said, passing scissors and wire to Celia and a bowl of roses that bore out her admission. "Look out for the thorns, Celia. The dark red ones are the worst."

Celia picked up a rose with care and buried her nose in its petals. With her face hidden, however inadequately, she felt at once safer, more able to deal with the other women. She could not be at ease with Miss Storace, whose kindness and penetration she feared, nor with Meg Lindsay for a different reason. From the shelter of her flower she permitted herself a positive statement.

"You are clumsy with flowers, Meg. You push them into the vase all anyhow."

"I am clumsy with everything. You should hear the little boys howl when I wash their grazes. I have to keep them quiet with peppermint creams."

"You are never clumsy with your own child."

Janet looked up, struck by the justice of this observation, and Celia reddened and turned away.

"It is time I put my own child to bed," Meg said. "When I have settled her I will lay the coffee trays in the library and see that the locker rooms are tidy."

"Will you just make sure that the first form girls all have clean dresses, and that they are suitable ones? Valerie Wells has knitted herself a shift in black and white, she assures me it is inspired by some man in Paris, but it is so short parents might think she borrowed a sweater from one of the boys and pulled it down as far as it would go. I don't want to hurt her feelings, but I wonder if she could find something else in her trunk?"

"I shall tell her a woollen dress would be too warm for July."

"Oh, what a good idea! But suppose it is miserably cold tomorrow?"

"It won't be. The forecast is warm, very warm, with a little rain towards evening."

"Good. Wet, cold Parents' Days are abominable. We have so many coming this year, I don't quite know why. A hundred and seventy mothers and fathers, countless younger brothers and sisters, and the usual handful of—" Janet stopped short, and Meg who was in the act of leaving the room was arrested by the

24

sudden faltering of that firm voice. Celia glanced up, Janet went on at once, "—of prospective customers. I never know what to call them, parents to be has quite the wrong connotations. Meg, I will come to the library with you, I think this bowl of sweet peas will look well on the table by the window."

Her tone forbade Meg to offer to take the bowl from her. Celia returned to her work with a sense of mystification, and the other women crossed the hall and went into the beautiful shabby library where a few children were still reading. Janet put down her sweet peas and called out,

"Clear the tables now, Diggory, Jane, Martin. Meg wants to lay the coffee trays. Some of you might like to go over to the studio and choose some little dishes for ashtrays. Make sure you ask who made them and get permission."

The children vanished, Meg said, "I will just find Clare and get her in the bath," but without conviction as she was now certain that Janet had something to say to her, and that it might not be anything that she would care to hear.

"Some people you know will be coming in the morning. I should have told you before, but you know how busy I have been."

Meg said nothing.

"It is Miss Lovat, Emma Lovat, that is how I always think of her, but of course you will remember her as Mrs. Branksome. Her husband will be with her, and their little boy." As Meg still said nothing Janet continued with an effect of gentle desperation, "He is just a little older than Clare, I believe."

"Yes, he must be," Meg said in a steady voice that concealed none of her inner disturbance from so practised an observer as Miss Storace. "Are they thinking of sending him here?"

"Emma thinks of it, her husband opposes the whole idea, but she hopes to bring him round. The child is awkward, is finding it difficulty to satisfy his teachers. They say he is gifted but lazy. His father thinks he is lazy."

"I am sorry for Mrs. Branksome," Meg said with a meaning that seemed to spring from another source than Janet's words.

"She asks me as an old friend to try to convince her husband that Cilrheddyn might be the right place for their boy : I don't know what influence she thinks I might be able to wield, if she has none. He will hardly be able to credit me with being dis-interested."

"Have they only the one child?"

"Yes, they were not young when they married."

"Then Mrs. Branksome must be very worried about him, to think of sending him away. She is not the sort of woman to shelve her responsibilities."

"We have very few mothers who might be said to come into that category," Janet said with some sharpness. "Such people generally balance their wish to be rid of their children against the cost of relief and decide that the loss to their bank balance would tie their hands as much as the presence of any child. Really rich people might be different, but Cilrheddyn does not cater for the really rich."

This was true and one good look around the library confirmed it. Everything from floor to ceiling needed painting or mending or simply replacing. The bright jackets of some recently added books cruelly exposed their dingy setting; but beyond the win-dows was sunshine, space, air with a sweet smell, flowers rather running to seed. Shouts could be heard from the tennis court and splashes from the pool, birdsong from the creeper that swathed and muffled this end of the house, and beneath, behind, beyond all other sounds, the notes of a clarinet losing themselves among the blackbirds' calls and the screams from the diving boards.

"We shall miss Jude next year," Janet said.

"Will Daniel Hardy be leaving too?"

"He may be. Has he spoken to you about it?"

"Not in so many words. I don't know what gave me the idea."

"He seems to have dropped hints in various places. We have heard nothing from his father, we have always assumed that he meant Dan to stay with us until he was ready for university. If there has been some change in their plans it might account for the strange way Daniel has been behaving this term."

Meg hardly knew that she had noticed Daniel's strange be-haviour, but eight years at Cilrheddyn had shown her how rarely Janet Storace saw more in a situation than was actually there, or softened the outlines of an impression to comfort herself or her brother. In the light of Janet's words small things came to her mind; though she spent very little time in the senior school as a rule, the loss of a matron this last term had added to her duties. Daniel, commended to her notice as a quiet reliable boy, had been perhaps less quiet than she had expected, and reliable was not a word she would have used of him herself. Nor when she came to think of it was that a word to fit most of the sixteen and seventeen year olds in the school : she pointed this out to Miss Storace now.

"My own brothers were rather wild at that age, I know my father used to worry over them a good deal."

"Yes, we have worried over Daniel ever since he came here; he was always under some constraint, he was a little too good to be true. Even as a first former he avoided fights and binges and any sort of escapade. But such a boy will usually begin to loosen up a little earlier than the fifth form, and often the loosening is rather drastic. Daniel has done nothing terrible, he is still a steady, quiet boy, only he is different and I would guess unhappy."

"I wonder where he is?" Meg now said, struck by a thought some hours old which had been buried deep in more pressing concerns. "I didn't see him at teatime. I am not even sure he was at lunch."

"Somebody would have mentioned it if he missed his afternoon lessons," Janet said, but seemed uncertain.

"Tess Pinnegar will know. She is hardly ever out of his sight. Shall I find her?"

"Yes, do that, Meg. And say nothing to alarm her : she is very fond of Daniel."

"His being fond of her wouldn't account for everything?"

"I hardly think so. Not here, not in the summer, when they can be so much together. And the girls make more of these things than the boys as a rule, the boys take their adoration for granted. They know they are adorable, their mothers adore them."

"Daniel has no mother, only a stepmother."

"Yes, that makes things no easier for him. All the same, being a little bit in love with Tess Pinnegar will do him no harm."

Children came back to them with misshapen pottery dishes and bowls on which the glaze had run.

"Will these do, Janet? They are all awful, Nancy says she will not have them on the pottery stall."

"Put one or two on each table, and some on the tops of the bookshelves. Diggory, where is your sister? Meg wants her."

Diggory said, "She is sitting on the terrace outside the music room, listening to Jude. Shall I fetch her?"

"No," Meg said. "I will come. Have you any garters, Diggory?"

"I lost them at the beginning of term. They are bad for the circulation."

"But good for the appearance," Janet said, with an eye on his legs. "See if anyone can lend you a spare pair. Just for one day they will hardly do you any harm."

"It is the principle of the thing," Diggory said as he went off with Meg. "We are always being told we should not sacrifice health to vanity but when the crunch comes you see what happens. Janet will wear high heels tomorrow," he predicted with contempt.

"Not very high. She never does."

"Her caution will outweigh her vanity; that is because she is as old as the hills."

"You exaggerate, Diggory."

"How old is she, Meg?"

"Twice as old as I am. Five times as old as you. With your gift for mathematics you should be able to work that out."

He worked it out, then burst into tuneless song.

> "Tess, Tess,
> Is the hell of a mess.
> She can't say no and won't say yes."

"What does that mean?" Meg said, stopping him with a hand lightly laid on his arm.

"Nothing. I made it up, Jude says it is about Tess and Daniel, and I made one up about Jude too. Shall I tell you that?"

"Would he like you to?"

> "Jude, Jude,
> Down in the wood,
> Doing something decidedly rude."

Diggory said, and looked sideways at Meg as if experimentally. She laughed, his brow cleared.

"I should like to write something about you, Diggory; but nothing rhymes with your name."

"That is the only good thing about it. Tamsin and I got the worst of my parents' passion for that man."

"Suppose they had called you Bathsheba and Gabriel?"

"I wonder if that is why Tess likes Daniel, because of the Hardy bit?"

"There are other things she might like him for. He is a fine looking boy."

"Yes, he has obvious good looks. Jude's and mine are more subtle. Mine are so subtle only I can see them."

"Run off now, Diggory. I can see Tess."

He obeyed without argument, rather to her relief. Meg was used to the smaller boys trotting at her heels when they were not congregated in flocks up trees or in ditches; she sometimes thought their steady presence might account for her own child's equally steady absence. A glance at her watch showed her that it was past Clare's bedtime. She called out, "Tess!" and the quick jerk with which the girl turned her head told her that her tone had been too sharp, almost peremptory. She softened it, all the more as she saw that the girl had been crying.

"Have you seen Daniel Hardy?"

"Not since this morning," Tess said, with a frightened look.

"Oh, Tess! Has anyone?"

"We were practising with him before lunch." And, as Meg made a movement towards the open window of the music room, "No, Meg, you mustn't interrupt them just now. It would be no use anyway. Jude doesn't know where he is."

Meg stood there undecided; the room beyond the window was velvety dark to her eyes. In a few moments she made out Tim, sitting down with his 'cello resting on his knees, and Jude, grim and abstracted, his brow wet with effort, releasing a stream of pearly semiquavers, rising, turning and falling with an effect of ease that his tense stance denied; Tess was right, that he must not be interrupted. She smiled at the girl, touching her gently on the shoulder for a reason that neither of them could have put a name to, and went in search of her daughter.

III

"THERE IS SOMETHING I should perhaps have told you before, Harry."

"Before Robert fell asleep?"

"No, it is something I would not mention while he was listening. But I might have told you years ago, I daresay you will think I have been very secretive."

He would not turn towards her while he was driving, but she sought his profile in some anxiety and thought he showed amusement. Certainly his next words were, for him, light enough.

"I daresay I will. Keeping anything to yourself for years is no part of my idea of you."

Emma Branksome felt herself blush for an accumulation of half-truths, for all those departures from an originally high standard of candour that care for her son had forced upon her. She had been outstandingly open, truthful almost to a fault, at the time of her marriage to Harry; she could not have foreseen the depths of disingenuousness she would require to plumb if Harry's home were to be made safe for a young child, or Robert's for his busy and brilliant father. To keep their separate rights clear in her aching head as she lovingly misrepresented each to the other with less and less success as time went by—this task had fatally rubbed the bloom off her peaceful conscience. That special secret she must now share with her husband seemed almost negligible in balance with those others on which, no matter what her inward cry, her lips must remain for ever closed.

"You will find," she said at last, "an old friend of ours at Cilrheddyn."

"Miss Storace, yes, I know. But, Emma, this secret of yours?"

"The secret is the old friend, and it is not Janet Storace, it is someone else, a good deal younger. We have not seen her for many years, I expect you will have forgotten her."

"I do not make friends so easily," he said drily, "that I am in any danger of forgetting those I do make."

"It was never a real friendship, hardly more than an acquaintance."

"You are tantalising, Emma! I don't know what I shall be imagining if you will not just say outright who it is."

"Well, then," Emma said with an effect of resignation, "it is Meg Lindsay."

For quite a long time he said nothing at all. This might have been accounted for by the state of the road, a steep gradient, the traffic, a change of gear. Emma knew it was not.

"It is not such a coincidence as it sounds," she said at last, and painfully.

"It cannot be. Coincidences are things of the moment, and you say you might have told me this years ago."

"I sent her there."

Now at last Harry did take his eyes off the road. Emma lowered her own and studied her hands.

"Six weeks after Robert was born I went back to see Mr. Medlicott; as I went into his consulting room Miss Lindsay came out. She had been crying. I thought nothing of it at the time, I had so much else to think about. A few days later she came to see me."

"I suppose she was pregnant," her husband said in a voice of cold disdain.

"Yes. She thought I had noticed, she thought I might have put two and two together—her affair with your brother-in-law, her visit to a gynaecologist, at his private address too, not at the hospital where she might have met you or Charles. She came to ask me not to tell Charles. She made me promise."

"Which you did readily enough, no doubt. You would never wish to make things hard for Charles. Women generally prefer to make things easier for him."

"I never thought of Charles. I thought of your sister; Julia would have been the one to suffer. You know how Charles contrives to escape suffering."

"Yes, I know. I see how you assist his escapes."

"I cannot tell you any more, Harry. It is like talking to a stone wall."

"A stone wall would be easier," Harry said, not without

humour. "I will spare you my comments. Tell me the rest of this story, and I will keep quiet until you finish."

Emma took courage, glanced at the back seat of the car to make sure that her son still slept, and went on.

"Well, then, I promised, and I asked her what she planned to do. I offered her money for an abortion."

"You did what!" Harry now cried.

"Yes, I was foolish, but I thought she could not want a baby. I thought it would be terrible for a baby to be born to a girl in her position. Of course I would not have given her your money, Harry, it would have been my own. And you need not worry, because she would not take it. I think perhaps she had been frightened by your sister's miscarriage a few weeks before: or perhaps she already knew she would love the child."

"She was an unusual girl," Harry said with an effect of re-calling from an immense distance a trivial perception. His wife knew that the perception could hardly have been so trivial, given the circumstances, and saw for a single bitter moment that marriage had perhaps compromised her husband's candour as well as her own. "Can there be no truth, then, where there is love?" some part of her cried out in disgust, while her lips spoke other words quite calmly.

"Yes, she was, more unusual even than we would have guessed. I asked her to keep in touch with me, I thought I might be able to help her, although I didn't see quite how, unless it were to pass on some of Robert's baby clothes; but when she did write to me at last it was to say she had refused to have her child adopted and was looking for a job: it wasn't easy, she had no special qualifications, and could I help her."

"Why you? Why not her parents?"

"She was the oldest of a large family, and her father was rector of a country parish. There was no money to spare, and I suppose Mr. Lindsay might have found some difficulty in explaining an illegitimate grandchild to his parishioners."

"I would have thought it a splendid chance for them to show a little practical Christianity."

"That is because you are not a churchgoer, Harry," Emma said with the nearest approach to ease she had made in the whole of this conversation. "In any case it is an academic point: she wouldn't go back to her family. She wanted a job with a home attached where she could keep the baby. She had applied for several as housekeeper, but the women who advertised seemed to think her too inexperienced."

"Or too experienced. Perhaps too attractive to be trusted."

"Yes, women would naturally think twice about taking anyone so striking into their homes. But I had a letter from Janet Storace complaining that she could never keep a junior matron for more than a few weeks, they were always leaving to get married. So I sent Miss Lindsay to her."

"And Miss Storace took her in?"

"At once and unconditionally. She is still there : her little girl will be nearly nine."

"And how does Miss Storace explain her to her pupils?"

Emma said carefully, "I think no explanations would be asked for."

"What does she call herself? Mrs. Lindsay? Of course it is easy enough to buy and wear a wedding ring."

"Janet and Matthew are called by their Christian names in the school," Emma said, with a catch of the breath as if his sudden vulgarity had caused her physical pain, "and so are all the staff. So I expect she is just Meg or Margaret, and children would not look for a wedding ring."

"I am glad to understand at last why they go in for this silly affected informality : it obviously makes things easier for any young woman who misbehaves herself."

"You had better stop the car," Emma cried in a spasm of anger. "If you have made up your mind to dislike the place and think the worst of my friends, what is the use of our going any further?"

"Keep your voice down," Harry said. "You will wake the boy."

"I am awake," the boy said in his harsh treble. "Are we going back to London?"

"No, we are not. We are in Wales already, I do not mean to drive back tonight."

"Is this Wales? It looks like everywhere else, only hillier. Where is Snowdon?"

"A long way away to the north," Emma said at once, before Harry could remark on his son's ignorance. "There are no mountains near Cilrheddyn, only hills, and the sea is not far away. The children spend whole days on the beach."

33

"Could we go to the sea tomorrow?"

"There won't be time."

"It seems a waste not to go, when we are so near."

"Yes, it does. Harry," Emma cried, forgetting her husband's mood in the sense of her son's disappointment, "could we stay another night and go to the sea on Sunday? Even if our hotel has no room for us there must be others. A day at the sea would do us all good."

"I daresay it would : I should like it myself. But I have an engagement on Sunday afternoon, and I must go to the Department on Sunday morning. My 'plane leaves for Copenhagen too early on Monday for me to see any of my patients or make arrangements for the week I shall be away"

"Are you going away again, Daddy?" Robert said with a note of joyous anticipation in his voice.

"Yes, to Copenhagen. Do you know where that is?"

"Somewhere abroad, because you are going by 'plane."

"That is very unsound reasoning," Harry said. "People fly to Manchester or Liverpool these days."

"People without cars. You would drive."

Emma felt the lurch of her fear for the boy, a sensation as familiar to her now as the dread she had once felt that Harry's wrath might be directed against herself. The silence that followed Robert's careful casual words seemed to all of them to last too long. Harry broke it, since Emma and her son dared not.

"Even if Cilrheddyn is the sort of earthly paradise your mother seems to think you won't find people there encouraging you to be insolent."

"Why was what I said insolent? It was true."

"It was the way you said it. You were trying to score off me."

"I was succeeding," Robert said, but not aloud.

"Say you are sorry, and it will all be over," Emma said, without any real hope that this would be so.

"I am sorry, sir."

"There is no need for you to call me sir. I have never asked for exaggerated signs of respect."

"The people you work with say sir. When I come to St. Chad's with you the sisters and the houseman all call you that."

"Sometimes they call me Professor Branksome."

"It would take too long if they all called you that every time."

"Yes, it would," Harry said, responding at last to what he thought was good sense on the boy's part. Emma alone detected the irony; when she looked over her shoulder at the child's face his eyes, dark and shadowed like his father's by heavy brows and a high, narrow forehead, met hers in an invitation to share the joke. Emma could not; she looked a reproach, the boy's eyes fell.

"I wish we could get to the sea," Harry said now, "but if we decide to send you to school here we will all go together next summer and perhaps take your friends with us."

This was so great a concession to her own ideas that Emma felt almost dizzy with gratitude. A scene averted, an advance made, the situation improved with such rapidity; she would not have dared hope for so much. And Harry was not capricious; for him to go as far as this meant nearly as much as a promise given. She began to see the loveliness of the land they passed through and to let it soothe her jangled nerves. Robert read the Welsh names on the signposts; neither his father nor his mother had any more idea than he how those names should be pronounced, so he was spared stern or loving correction. His spirits rose, he began to sing; as they drove over the Teifi into Newcastle Emlyn the sight of a county boundary post sent him into fits of laughter. "Sir Benfro! Sir Benfro!" he shouted, rolling about in the back seat.

"People who live in Pembrokeshire may not find it so funny," Harry said as he stopped the car outside their hotel.

"Pembrokeshire, is that what it means? I see, Sir is shire and Benfro is Pembroke. I know two words of Welsh."

"Yes, you are not completely incapable of learning," Harry said. "Now calm down; we cannot take you into the hotel while you are making that noise."

His mother's face rather than his father's words quietened the child. He got out of the car and stood on the pavement.

"Look, Robert, that must be one of the boys from Cilrheddyn," Emma said while Harry fumbled in the boot for overnight cases.

"It isn't a boy, it is nearly a man."

To Emma it was a boy; she recognised the blue shirt and drill shorts from the illustrated brochure Janet had sent her. But Daniel Hardy was tall, and must seem taller to Robert who was under the usual size for his age in spite of his father's height and Emma's heavy build.

"Yes, he must be in the sixth form, I should think."

Harry's eyes followed their gaze, and his tone when he spoke was incredulous.

"Their sixth formers come down to the town in the evening and prop up the lamp-posts like any young hooligan?"

Emma could think of no answer except that Daniel did not look like any young hooligan; she suppressed this opinion and followed Harry into the cool dark hall of the hotel, almost pulling Robert after her. "Robert, you must come along. We have to get tidy before dinner. You will be late for bed."

"It won't hurt him for once," Harry said, "and he had better get used to laxity and irregularity if that is how you think he should be educated."

A state primary school and two day preparatory schools had failed so far to educate his son: Emma did not point this out. That Robert could read Sir Benfro on a road sign was little thanks to any of those institutions: the same words in a book would have defeated him. She picked up the case that held her own things and the boy's and followed the receptionist upstairs. Two rooms side by side at the end of a passage were reserved for them: one contained twin beds, the other was a single room. Robert ran ahead of Emma into the first of these.

"May I have the bed by the window?"

"The other room is yours," Harry said from the doorway. "We shall not be coming up to bed until later, and you would be disturbed."

"When you are away I often sleep in your bed. I don't wake up when Mummy gets in, do I, Mummy?"

Emma said helplessly, "Sometimes you do. You need a good night's sleep if you are to have a pleasant day tomorrow."

"I am not tired: I slept in the car."

"You are not to argue," Harry said quietly enough. "Take your things into your own room, wash your hands and face and change your shirt."

Again it was Emma's face rather than Harry's voice that sent the child away, but not before both his parents had seen the dusky flushing of his cheeks and the twisting of his mouth.

"Harry, we are in a strange place—"

"Our home is not a strange place when I am away. The boy winds you around his little finger, he gets his own way from

36

morning till night. And this is the child you think of sending to a boarding school!"

"It is just because what you say is true," Emma said, shaking out her nightdress with a movement that was not quite under control. "That is the very reason he should go, Harry."

"Because he is too attached to you, do you mean?"

Her husband sat upon his bed, watching the woman he had married, perhaps too late, as she moved about the room putting a hairbrush here, a handbag there. "Or because he is afraid of me, Emma?"

She came back from the dressing table and sat beside him.

"A little of both, I think. It is all wrong, Harry, it is terrible that he should be so pleased when you are to go off for a few days."

"If you are beginning to be pleased too, then, yes, it is terrible."

Her silence answered him truthfully. He put his arm around her, not without tenderness, and his next words were tender enough.

"Have you asked yourself what hell he will go through, sleeping in a dormitory with other boys, nearly two hundred miles away from you? I have been through it, I was wretched for the first weeks of every term; after that I was hopeless, knowing there was no help for it."

"Cilrheddyn was not like the prep school you went to, Harry, or like your public school."

"But it is still not home. If he wants you and cries for you, will you still feel it is right for him, just because you cannot hear him crying?"

"Other people might be able to comfort him. At this place I know they would try. They would not put him off with cant about being a brave boy, or believe in their own hearts that it was good for his character to suffer so."

"Yes, that would be a difference," Harry said, almost to himself as his son appeared in the doorway looking fresh and neat; almost a handsome child in spite of reddened eyes and a resentful chin.

"Yours is a nice room, Robert," Emma said cheerfully, "and it will be quieter at night than this one which overlooks the main street. Now let us have dinner and then I will come up with you and read a bedtime story."

Robert had crossed to the window.

"That boy is still there, he is just standing about all the time. Oh, look, Mum, a super car! Is it a Jaguar?"

Emma joined him with an apologetic smile at Harry. The car was not, she thought, a Jaguar, but certainly it was impressive. Her eye was drawn by a movement across the street; the boy in the blue shirt had darted into the alleyway between two shops.

"He is on the run," Robert cried, with a sharp intake of breath. "He is hiding from the law! You watch, there are secret agents in that car!"

Harry came over, drawn by the excitement in the child's voice. The car had stopped under their very window, but the man who got out of it could not have looked less like a spy; he was too noticeable, there was too much of him. As tall as, or taller than Harry or the boy in the blue shirt, he wore a golden beard, only a little brighter than his hair. He opened the passenger door, a dark and charming woman climbed out and immediately turned to let another passenger out of the back. The man's offices were also necessary; he took a stick, a handbag, a parcel. Then an old lady, at first sight frail, joined them on the pavement.

"Your secret agents are pretty well disguised, Robert," Harry said.

"But the boy is hiding from them, Harry. Robert was right about that."

"Perhaps they are his parents."

"That girl could not be his mother, nor could the old lady. I don't know why we are staring at them, it is none of our business. Robert, come away from the window."

They left the room, Robert with some reluctance and a last glance over the street. There was no sign of the boy.

"He is a fugitive all right. He was afraid of that man with the beard."

"Nonsense," Harry said, taking his son's hand firmly. "My theory is the most likely. The man with the beard is his father; the boy would not be running away from his own father. He is playing some sort of game."

"It is a strange time to choose to run away," Janet Storace said, "if that is what Daniel is doing. He will see his parents tomorrow; at his age waiting a few hours shouldn't be impossible."

"He is nowhere in the house, Janet, and nobody has seen him anywhere in the grounds. Jude was the last person to speak to him but he is with Tim in the music room practising for the concert, so I came away. Tess could tell me nothing."

"Well, thank you, Meg dear, for what you have done : I will speak to my brother. You will want to be getting to bed, Clare. It will be a long day tomorrow. There is a little boy coming you might like to look after : he is only a few months older than you."

"I don't like boys much. There are more of them than girls."

"That is generally so at boarding schools."

"Why?" Clare asked her mother as they went off together. "Don't their mothers and fathers like them so much?"

"Of course they do. But they are sometimes harder to manage."

"Because they are bigger and rougher?"

"Perhaps."

"If I were a boy would you have sent me to a boarding school?"

"I don't suppose I would have had the money."

"If I had an ordinary father?"

"Perhaps. There are so many things parents have to worry about; choosing a school is just one of them."

"Tess says she came here because she was ill."

"Yes, and so did some of the others."

"I thought people went to hospital when they were ill and doctors looked after them, not teachers. Perhaps they come here because you are nearly a doctor."

"Get your dress off, Clare. I am not nearly a doctor : I was a medical student once before you were born. I cannot look after people when they are ill, I would not know what to do for them."

"If you were a real doctor would you have enough money to send me away to school?"

"I wish you wouldn't ask so many questions," Meg said in a voice much colder than any she normally used to her child.

"Well, would you?"

Meg swallowed the words that came to her lips before they could do the damage that threatened. "If you had never been born, then I would be a doctor now." This was not the full truth for Meg had abandoned her professional training before she had known herself to be pregnant, but it was near enough to the truth to require suppressing.

"I don't know," she said, feebly, it seemed to both of them. "I am going to run your bath. You must hurry, Clare, the Form One boys will be up in ten minutes."

"They can wait," Clare said. "They don't really want baths, showers would do."

"All of them are bathing tonight," Meg said. "You must leave your hot water."

"I will leave my germs in it," Clare said with satisfaction. "How disgusted their mothers would be if they knew."

"They would be a lot more disgusted if the fees had to go up to pay for a new hot water system," Meg said, and then, with emphasis, "Clare, hurry! Am I ever going to get you into bed tonight?"

"I wonder where Daniel will sleep?"

"He will come back at bedtime. Janet is right, he won't have run away when his people will be here tomorrow. If he went home there would be nobody there, he is old enough to remember that."

"Daniel has a step-mother. Oh, how hot the water is—can I have some cold?"

"Not too much, or the Form One boys won't be able to get their knees clean."

"If you married now I should have a step-father."

"Yes," said Meg.

"And little step-brothers and sisters."

"Perhaps."

"They would be younger than me, but I would be the Cinderella one."

"I never thought of it; perhaps the Ugly Sisters were younger than Cinderella."

"No, they were old and ugly. That is what their name means. Where is my toothbrush?"

"In Richard's mug."

"Has it been rubbing against his? Will it have his germs on it?"

"If it has they will do you no harm. Richard is perfectly well."

"Doctors are supposed not to like germs."

"I am not a doctor," Meg said, for the second time in twenty minutes. Her child heard the exasperation in her voice and applied herself to brushing her teeth. The Form One boys waited outside in variously vocal degrees of impatience. When she emerged, rather pink herself in a pink dressing gown, they emitted eleven year old wolf whistles. Clare accepted these as her due, and walked past with an indifferent grace that was at once an echo and a loving parody of her mother's.

IV

TESS PINNEGAR, HER friends Nancy and Kate, all girls between seventeen and nineteen, lay on their beds in the dormitory where they slept when the weather was too cold for them to be in their tents at the edge of the school orchard. They had come inside to escape the gnats, and to prepare themselves in various ways for the morrow. The windows of the room faced west, the sun flooded in and so did Celia's voice calling the younger children in to bath.

"I wish I had washed my hair this afternoon," Kate said: she had a looking glass in her hand and studied herself in it, spreading her hair over the pillow with her brush.

"It looks clean enough."

"It doesn't feel clean. My scalp itches."

"Wash it now," Tess said. "If you lean out of the window it will be dry by bedtime."

"I've run out of shampoo."

"You can have some of mine. Some of Jude's, rather. I have been using his for weeks now."

"Thanks, but I don't think I will. Brushing will liven it up. A pimple is coming on my chin."

"If you cannot think of anything but your appearance," Nancy said, "could you just very kindly shut up, Kate? Because some of us, I mean me, are trying to work."

Kate said fretfully, "People say you should never squeeze pimples, but what else can one do? There!"

"You have made it bleed," Tess said. "Have a handkerchief."

"Is that Jude's too?" her friend said, taking it.

"Yes, I always lose mine: then I start losing his."

"Do you think your brother is all a boy should be, Tess?" Kate now said, dabbing at her chin with this boy's handkerchief and inspecting the results with love.

"Whatever do you mean by that?"

"What would you expect her to mean?" Nancy said, putting down her book. "She means that Jude is impervious to her charms, so she wonders if he can be sexually immature for his age."

"I am sure Jude thinks you are very pretty, Kate."

"Thank you for nothing. I know he is not blind."

"But he is too busy with music to have much time for girls."

"Musical people need a great deal of sex. I read a book that made that point."

"If there were such a book," Nancy said, "Kate would certainly have read it."

"Liszt was as sexy as anything. Women screamed and swooned at his recitals."

"Was that in the same book or another one?"

"Another one. Or a magazine or something. And think of Wagner, all that Tristan stuff."

"She is better educated than anyone would guess, looking at her," Nancy said to Tess. "She has read a book and a magazine or something, and she knows that Wagner wrote an opera about Tristan. Her parents are getting a return for their money, the existence of Cilrheddyn is justified."

"The bleeding has stopped," Kate said, and sat up to give Tess back her handkerchief : her hair, thick, fine and fair reached halfway down her back. She picked up her looking glass again.

"These holidays I shall have it cut very short like Meg's."

"It is a shame Meg cut her hair," Tess said eagerly. "It was beautiful and there was so much of it."

"It is still beautiful, the colour is what counts with her. Do you think Matthew and Janet would have a fit if I came back with hair that colour?"

"Red out of a bottle is a different colour altogether. And, no, neither of them would have a fit; Matthew would look hurt and Janet would say it looked very nice, how brave of you to try something new, and they would both wonder why you disliked yourself so much you wanted to go around in disguise."

"I wish you were a little less clever, Nancy."

"I wish you were a little more clever, Kate."

Kate lay back and brushed her hair out again.

"It looks like the rays of the sun in my baby sister's paintings," Tess said.

"When will she be coming here, Tess?"

"Not for another year. She is only nine."

"She looks more like you than Jude. And more like Diggory too."

"Yes, we are all thin and dark like my mother. And Jude is thick and dark like my father."

"You would not think to look at Jude that he was gifted in any way."

"There has to be some justice," Nancy said. "Imagine if you had talent as well as beauty! Or if I had Tess's shape and my brains."

"Your shape is very nice, Nancy, and there are special bras you can get to help."

"Are there really?" Nancy said in the mocking tone she used to disguise her affection for Tess and to reveal her deep disapproval of Kate.

"This year will be your last Parents' Day, Nancy," Kate now said, turning her head to right and left in an attempt to gauge the length of her eyelashes. "And next year will be the last for Tess and me. We shall all disperse and probably never see each other again."

"We can come back to reunions."

"We could bring our boy friends," Kate said, in a light tone.

"Those of us who have any."

"You will have boy friends, Nancy," Tess said. "There are sure to be lots of very clever boys at Cambridge and then you will be appreciated."

"As I am not here, even by the very clever boys."

"Jude is not so very clever," Kate said.

"I hope you are not falling in love with Jude," Tess said. "It is such a waste, when he is leaving at the end of the term."

"I should like to make his last days here happy," Kate said with a deep sigh.

"I think he is rather happy already. And what about Peter? You would be spoiling his last days if you deserted him for Jude."

"Oh, Peter. I wish I had learnt the piano. Then I could play Jude's accompaniments."

"Who would have thought Kate's mind could harbour such a pure notion?"

"When I fall in love," Kate said in a deeper voice than usual which seemed to admonish Nancy for her levity, "I shall hope to share all my lover's interests."

"You will," Nancy said, "as long as he is interested in you."

"I daresay it sounds rather oldfashioned, but I think a woman should be prepared to make sacrifices. When the time comes for me to give myself I shall give my mind as well as my body."

"Whatever will anyone do with her *mind*?" Nancy said to Tess. "Can she be thinking of the plastic daffodils they give away with packets of detergent?"

"One danger of looking as I do," Kate said, raising herself on her elbow, "is that I may be thought to be frivolous or shallow. But I honestly believe that I am capable of great devotion."

"As long as you believe it," Nancy said.

"I think I will wash my head after all, Tess. Using Jude's shampoo will be the next best thing to feeling him running his fingers through my hair."

"You had better borrow my drier too," Nancy said, shutting her book with a snap. "Perhaps the current of warm air will be the next best thing to Jude's hot breath on your cheek."

"You may pretend to be cynical," Kate said in a very sweet way, "but Florence says you are just the sort of girl to struggle for years against the springs of passion in your own nature, and then to abandon yourself utterly and perhaps end up as a prostitute."

"Saints preserve us!" Nancy said. "What book or magazine did Florence get that out of?"

"I can't remember. Do you think it would be D. H. Lawrence?"

"After six years of living with her I still find Kate capable of surprising me," Nancy said to Tess, and got off her bed. "Now I must round up the second formers and hound them off to bed."

"I heard Celia calling them twenty minutes ago"

"They take no notice of Celia: she is too kind to them, she almost apologises to them for having to do her job."

"I am sure you are not too kind, Nancy," Kate said.

"No, I tell them that if they are not in and out of the bath in five minutes I will smack their bottoms."

"What would Matthew say if they told him?"

"They do tell him, they like it very much. It adds a spice of danger to their well-regulated lives."

"But do you, actually? Smack them?"

"I would if the need arose," Nancy said. "Threats should never be idle."

"Mother has gone to bed," Dinah Hardy said when she joined her husband in the lounge of the hotel. "She is tired, so tired that she was ready to admit it. I will take her in a nightcap later and make sure that she is comfortable."

"You are very good to her, Dinah."

"Well, since we have to live together, paying her these little attentions does help to make things easier; and I don't want her to be difficult tomorrow. Dealing with Daniel will be hard enough without that."

"You must leave Daniel to me. He has never been unreasonable before, I am sure he will understand our feelings now, once we really have a chance to talk things over."

"Vincent, it is half past eight: is there a television set? Would anybody mind, do you think?"

"There is just that one man, reading. I will ask him if you like."

Vincent Hardy went up to the one man and coughed to attract his notice. Harry Branksome looked up and recognised the bearded man from the big car.

"Should you be disturbed if we turned on the television? There is a serial my wife and I make a point of watching each week."

"By all means turn it on. It won't worry me."

"Thank you very much. Dinah, he doesn't mind; I will switch on, and we shall only have missed the first few minutes."

The serial turned out not to be one of the two that Harry had heard of. It was not set in a hospital, which would have set his teeth on edge, nor in a Northern working class street ripe for demolition, but in what he made out, after some moments, to be a school, a very modern school, co-educational like Cilrheddyn; large, unlike Cilrheddyn. The staff seemed mostly to be young, good looking, full of healthy enthusiasm and bursting with ideals: they seldom opened their mouths without allowing one or two of these to pop out. There were however older teachers, distrustful, pragmatic, openly nostalgic for the days of corporal punishment and impositions. The headmaster—even Harry realised that a headmistress would somehow have been more appropriate—was a sort of saint. In the course of thirty-five minutes he dealt successively and successfully with a threatened fire in the physics laboratory, a paranoid father claiming damages for an imagined assault on his son, a tearful young teacher—even prettier and fuller of ideals than the rest— afraid that one of the sixth form had written her an obscene letter, and what appeared to be a chronic mystery centred on the disappearance of books from the library of the history department. From time to time Vincent and his wife sought and caught each other's eyes, nodded, smiled. Sometimes their appreciation was verbal.

"I thought Frank did that awfully well, Vincent. How extraordinary that such a gentle creature should bluster so beautifully when he has to."

"Good production, I rather think. Frank starts off every rehearsal far too mild and reasonable, but John soon gets him loosened up. And I do honestly think the quality of the dialogue helps."

"That scene between him and the Head, what hours it took to get that right! It would be so easy to slip over into caricature, to make him into a sort of contemporary Squeers."

"Yes, but that's just where having Frank play the part is so splendid, don't you see? His real gentleness counteracts the beastly things you make him say."

Harry was not trying to listen, was almost trying not to listen, but the Hardys did not lower their voices and their enthusiasm carried as far as their words. At the end of the programme they switched the set off, then apologised and asked him if he wanted to see the news. He did not, he preferred a morning paper. They sat in their strange, stiff hotel armchairs looking at him expectantly: he did not in the least know what they were expecting.

"You didn't find it too trying?"

"It wasn't absolutely an ordeal?"

"The programme you were watching? No."

"But you didn't actually enjoy it?"

That they were in some way connected with what he had seen Harry could not have failed to make out: but he was not very skilled in the subtler forms of tact and where many men would have said oh, yes, very much, and given the matter no further

47

thought, Harry could only manage, "I found it interesting, but far-fetched."

"Oh, far-fetched? In what way?"

"Everybody seemed rather too good to be true, unless they were too bad to be true."

"Oh, that," Vincent said in a tone of relief. "They have to be, you know. The mass audience. We would like more subtlety, wouldn't we, Dinah? We originally conceived the thing in altogether different terms, much more esoteric and provocative, but they wouldn't look at it."

"And as long as they wouldn't look at it," Dinah said with eager frankness, "the viewing public couldn't look at it either. So we took our scripts back and really got to work on them. We went through them with a fine tooth comb for anything, anything at all that people might find puzzling."

"Scepticism, ambiguity, reservations, you know, the tongue in cheek lark—that doesn't go down very well at all, not at the popular viewing hours. Sincerity is the sine qua non. You have to believe in what you write, you have to bear witness."

"You wrote the—the play we have just seen?" Harry said, with a sense of venturing into foreign waters.

"I write most of it," Dinah said with her charming smile and a faint blush, "and then Vincent tidies it up and makes sure it has the right total ambience."

"He makes sure it is sincere?"

The Hardys laughed; their laughter implied that they were much more sophisticated than Harry, so sophisticated that they had come out the far side of cynicism and could afford to be in favour of belief.

"Yes, I suppose I do just that; and I think I add that note of deeper psychological insight the critics like so much. You may have seen what Richardson said in the *Observer* two Sundays ago—"

"My wife might have," Harry said as Emma came in. "I get very little time to read reviews and that sort of thing. Emma, I have been watching a play on television."

"Not a play," Vincent said smoothly, and rose to clear magazines from a chair so that Emma could sit down. "A serial. Called 'Comprehensive.' The title was Dinah's own. I thought it rather stark at first; lacking in human interest which they regard as

48

important, but it seems to have caught the public attention."

"These clever people," Harry said in mild desperation, "are writers, Emma. They wrote the play—the serial I have just seen."

"The episode," Dinah said with her little breathless air of pity. "Do you think you will want to watch the next one?"

"Oh, come, Dinah, that is very unfair!" Vincent roared, but waited for Harry's answer.

"I shall be in Denmark this time next week," Harry said. "Well, Emma, is Robert asleep?"

"Was that your little boy in the dining room?" Dinah said to Emma.

"Yes, and he is not asleep. He finds it hard to settle in a strange place."

"He is a very striking child, isn't he? My husband's son, my stepson, is handsome too; that is really one reason why we sent him to school down here. He is not so very much younger than I am, and it would be too sad if anything like Phédre developed."

"That was only one of the reasons," Vincent said while Emma glanced at Harry in alarm, which her husband's ignorance of Racine made quite superfluous. "Daniel is a bright boy who needed more individual attention than he would get at an ordinary grammar school."

"Oh, that is just like Robert!" Emma said. "Is your son at Cilrheddyn, then? We have come down to see the Storaces and make up our minds if Robert should come here."

Vincent looked at his wife triumphantly—it was impossible to mistake the "I told you so" quality of his look : such a look seemed to Dinah to need some explanation, and she addressed herself to Harry.

"I was quite wrong about you. Vincent said you were down here for that as soon as you came into the dining room, and I said no, you didn't look a bit like Cilrheddyn parents, especially you!"

"Really we ought to introduce ourselves : Dinah always overwhelms people with confidences and forgets they do not even know her name. I am Vincent Hardy, this is my wife Diana, the old lady with us is Mrs. Daintry, my first wife's mother."

"My name is Branksome," Harry said, seeing no help for it, "and my wife's name is Emma."

A little pause followed during which both women and one of the men wondered if it were possible that the other people could be ignorant of the extraordinary good fortune they were enjoying in being admitted with such ease to the company of the well known. Harry did not share these thoughts. He had no doubts about his own reputation, but he was well aware that to most people his name would mean nothing. That Vincent was a writer, and apparently a successful one had been established for him some time before. He did not think writers in general of much importance.

"Why don't we look like Cilrheddyn parents?" Emma asked Dinah. "Is there a special look?"

"Well, just look at us! We typify it, don't we, Vincent?"

"Speak for yourself. I typify nothing."

"The fathers are not all bearded?"

"Very few of them," Dinah said with a glance at her husband's splendid head, "but they do tend to have rather a lot of hair; perhaps because they are not the sort of people who wear bowler hats to the office every day."

Her eyes turned to Harry: his hair though hardly as bright and luxuriant as Vincent's was not noticeably thin.

"What sort of people are they, then? Is it possible to generalise?"

"Only in a negative way," Vincent said. "They are not rich, they are not poor; they are not worldly, but they are not Bohemian, either. They profess great admiration for freedom of expression, and get into a state when they see their children's examination results. They are all in favour of birth control and abortion law reform, and are scrupulously faithful to their lawful wedded spouses. They hope that the school is small because not many people think along such advanced lines as themselves and they are afraid that it is small because it is a failure."

Emma's face showed her dismay, and Dinah laughed, but kindly, and put out her hand.

"Vincent is teasing you, we both take a childish delight in shocking our friends. Won't you come through to the bar and have a drink with us?"

Harry looked up in alarm, then encountered Emma's eyes, turned hopefully to him.

"Thank you, I should like to if Emma is not too tired."

"Oh, I am not a bit tired. I will just slip upstairs first and make sure that Robert has got off to sleep. Don't wait for me, I will join you in a few minutes."

Vincent ordered whisky for himself and Harry, and vodka for his wife.

"Can you guess what Mrs. Branksome would like, or should I wait and ask her?"

"Emma scarcely ever drinks. I think she would like something long and cool."

"Mrs. Branksome," Vincent said, as Emma came in, "your husband says you would like something cool and he implies that it should contain very little alcohol. Is he right?"

"Yes. No. He would be right, but I had better not have anything at all. Harry, Robert says that he has had a nightmare. He is crying, I think I had better stay with him."

"I will go," Harry said and drained his glass. "You sit down and enjoy your drink, whatever it is to be. Thank you, Hardy. Good night, Mrs. Hardy. I shall see you tomorrow."

"Are you sure, Harry?" Emma said in a desperate undertone that was not lost upon their new friends.

"Of course I am. Robert will have you in and out of his room all night if you go back now. He knows I will stand no nonsense."

Emma looked after him with a sad sense of helplessness : she had so nearly forgotten Vincent that when he handed her something clear and colourless in a tall glass with a wisp of lemon peel on the top she looked at him and at her drink with something nearer panic than pleasure.

"What a shame for you!" Dinah said. "Aren't children the very devil sometimes? It is just as well I have none, I am far too selfish to be a good mother. You will meet some splendid mothers tomorrow, women who are hardly there at all : you look at them and right through them and what you see is their children. You listen to what they say and what you hear is the voice of their son or daughter or some of each. Like Helen Pinnegar, she is the most of all. She is like the man in the James story, the one who just disappears when there is no one around to admire him—except that admiration means nothing to Helen, she only wants her family to have some use for her. I told her a year ago she would have a terrible time at the menopause, women like her always do, and she said she was going to evening classes and extramural lectures and brushing up her shorthand and typing. I had a feeling she was going to burst into tears at any moment so I said something nice about Tess or Jude, or perhaps it was Diggory, it was exactly as if I had given her a shot in the arm, wasn't it, Vincent?"

"Exactly," Vincent said. He said to Emma, "Dinah is not without mercy, as you see. First a blow below the belt, then a shot in the arm. But she has a very good heart in spite of all evidence to the contrary. She is wonderful to Daniel, and very forbearing to my first wife's mother. Could one ask more of a woman than that?"

Emma smiled over the rim of her glass, hoping he did not want an answer and not knowing what answer he could want. She was aware that Dinah's fearless eyes were on her face; she was sure that Dinah's quick mind knew what to make of her, of Robert, of Harry. In some story or other Dinah would have read of a woman like herself, who would have liked to be a splendid mother but had come to the job too late, too little prepared, too full of fear. She finished her drink, said some pleasant things in an absent way, and escaped at the first opportunity. On the way upstairs she passed one of the chambermaids, a dark girl, pretty in a way that might have been Welsh but was not; her accent came from further afield.

"I have been with your little boy, he was crying. His father was cross with him, I think. But he has gone to sleep now, I gave him some milk and he was very tired."

"He will never drink milk when I give it to him," Emma said, and then, lest this sounded ungracious, "thank you very much. I would have come earlier if I had known."

She looked in at Robert and saw for herself that he slept. Then she went to her husband; in the few steps between the doors of the two bedrooms she prepared some words of remonstrance, thought better of them, and buried in her heart another chance for harsh speeches and second thoughts, for rage and reconciliation.

V

"Is there anything I can do for you, Meg?" Celia Spurgeon said, as if there really might be, though Meg was sitting alone in the staff room with a book and her knitting and gave no sign of needing help with either of these occupations.

"No, I have finished for the day. I put the third form boys on their honour to bath and get into bed by themselves."

"Who is going to sleep with them if Daniel Hardy is not back?"

"Isn't he back?" Meg said, putting down her book.

"Tess Pinnegar says not, she has been up and down stairs all evening looking for him."

"Then I shall have to tell Janet. I suppose Jude could come into the dormitory."

"Oh, not Jude, Meg! He does so love to sleep outside!"

Meg caught much more in Celia's words and tone than there was any need for them to hold, and was puzzled by this young woman's vehemence.

"It will do him no harm to come in for once: and there is no one else. The rest of the fifth form boys all have a dormitory to supervise already. Jude wriggled out of that job as he wriggles out of everything else he doesn't want to do."

"That is very unfair, Meg! He does his share of chores, he helped Matthew in the rock garden yesterday, he practically put up the platform in the music room single-handed."

"So that the parents could get a better view of him," Meg said without rancour. "Jude is a past master at getting his own way, and everyone forgives him because of his talent. He will begin to think he is beyond criticism if nobody ever reminds him that he still has something to learn."

"Why are you always finding fault with him, Meg?"

"Why are you always making excuses for him, Celia?" Meg said, but not as if she expected any answer. "Somebody must sleep in the third form dormitory, and it will have to be Jude."

"I will go and tell him," Celia said, with a look that seemed to beg for Meg's indulgence. "Where would he be, do you think?"

"An hour ago he was practising with Tim in the Music Room."

"They are not there any longer. Tim is altering the programmes for the concert."

"He may be in his tent already," Meg said. "It is only just nine but he probably wants an early night with such a day ahead of him."

Celia looked at her reproachfully and went off to the orchard on the east side of the house where a dozen tents or more, green, orange, blue and varying shades of white were set up in two separate clusters. To Kate who sat on the grass shaving her legs with a battery razor she called, "Have you seen Jude?"

"Yes, he is in his tent. Shall I get him for you?"

"Thank you, I can manage."

"Oh, hell," Jude said ungracefully when Celia told him why she had come. "I wanted a good night's sleep."

"I am awfully sorry, but Meg says there is nobody else."

"Couldn't the wretched brats sleep by themselves just for once?"

"They wouldn't sleep at all. They get so excited the night before Parents' Day: you would think they hadn't seen their fathers and mothers for years on end."

"Why should they sleep any better if I am there?"

"They will lie quiet at least and get some rest. It is no use arguing, Jude. I told Meg you preferred to sleep outside but she says you must come in."

"Meg is as hard as nails," Jude said with grudging approval. "Must I come over now?"

"I think so," Celia said apologetically. "Nine o'clock is their bedtime, and if you show them you mean business they will settle before you want to go to bed yourself."

"Perhaps Daniel will be back by ten. He will have to sleep somewhere."

"Nobody seems to be very worried about Daniel," Celia said as if this fact had only just struck her. "Of course it is none of my business, but I should have thought the police ought to be told."

"The police?" Jude said, with a look of alarm. "Why on earth?

He is not a child, or even a girl. And he will not die of exposure on a July night in Pembrokeshire, not even if he sleeps under a hedge."

"No, I suppose not. His parents would be upset, though, if they knew he had run away."

"Oh, run away! That is what first and second formers do: Daniel did not like something I said to him this afternoon and went off in a huff. He will get over it, it was no surprise to him."

"Then it is your fault he has gone?" Celia said, in an odd way, which seemed almost to contain a little pride at Jude's achievement along with dismay at its possible consequences.

"What I said was no more than the truth," Jude said, and began to gather together some books, his pyjamas, a sponge-bag. "How he took it is his own business." He saw that Celia did not like simply to ask what this truth had been and made a concession to her diffidence; this was about as near generosity as the boy could come with a woman who took so painful and pitiful an interest in him. "Tim knows all about it," he said, with what she took to be stifled impatience, and strolled off towards the house, throwing back at her, "You might ask him, if you like."

"I suppose mercy is a quality one should not look for in boys of Jude's age," Janet said to Tim, who had gone to her as soon as they finished practising and he had sent Jude away. "Of course he may have thought Daniel was too phlegmatic to take such an attack to heart; very touchy people are so quick to assume nobody else has feelings to be hurt."

"Jude has told him before how badly he plays, and Daniel has always made a joke of it."

"But today it was not a joke, so either Jude meant more than he has meant at other times or Daniel for some reason could stand less. I wonder if I should see Jude."

"I don't think it would do any good. I hinted to him that he might have been kinder, that there are some things better not said, but of course he knew that already. Look at Tess, she is good nature itself; and even Diggory, he is blunt and sometimes malicious, but he would not attack anyone as Jude attacked Daniel. It is not just a matter of their personalities clashing or their age or anything like that, it is—" the young man hesitated, flushed, and finally mumbled, "—it is something we all pay lip service to in theory; and in practice it is so ugly we can hardly recognise it."

"If you are trying to say that Jude possesses artistic integrity," Janet said severely, "that is no news to any of us : but there is a time and a place for everything, even that, and the afternoon before Parents' Day is the wrong time."

Tim burst out laughing, and only a moment passed before Janet laughed too, and they were still laughing when Celia tapped cautiously on the door of Janet's pleasant sitting room. She came in, her face lightening at the sight of their cheerful faces but the conclusion she drew from so much cheerfulness was as usual wrong.

"Daniel has turned up, then? Everything is all right?"

"No," Janet said, and rose from her chair, "he has not turned up and everything is very wrong, and now I shall have to go and tell Matthew all about it. There is some fresh fruit on the sideboard, Celia. Help yourself and give Tim some; I believe it is getting warmer, not colder, as the sun goes down."

"Janet is right," Tim said, taking a peach from the bowl Celia proffered. "The wind has dropped. Nobody will get much sleep tonight."

"Jude will be in the third form dormitory, Meg insisted on it. I hope he won't be any the worse for it tomorrow."

"If he played just about half as well as usual he would still show the rest of us up for the amateurs we are. That should satisfy you."

"I wasn't thinking of my own satisfaction. He would not like to fall below his usual standard."

"He has fallen below Janet's today," Tim said with some amusement.

"Because he was unkind to Daniel?"

"There is unkindness and unkindness. Janet is not much bothered by the ordinary kind. Jude is a virtuoso of the savage tongue; it is not a gift Janet wishes him to foster."

"It is a good thing his father can take Daniel's place," Celia said with a defeated air, as it now became clear to her that nobody would tell her what Jude had said to Daniel, or what tone he had used, or how he had looked saying words too awful, apparently, to be repeated.

"He will have to do better than that, if he doesn't want to find himself in Daniel's shoes."

"Oh, Tim! Jude is not a monster!"

"No, he only has the makings of a fine egotist. His father would not relish that any more than Janet does."

"He is hardly more than a child in some ways. Mr. Pinnegar would understand that, since Jude is his child, and he is a teacher as well as a father."

Tim looked at her with affectionate concern.

"He has a very moving apologist in you, Celia. I should like to think you would stand up for me as bravely if I were in disgrace."

But she almost stamped her pretty foot, and quite shook her neat little head.

"Jude is not in disgrace, he is just a boy in a state of conflict."

"Poor little Celia," Tim said with a snort of laughter, which he suppressed almost at once. "Don't let Janet hear you talking case-workers' jargon. That boy in a state of conflict feels no remorse and wants no pity. You heard him play earlier this evening; did it strike you then that he had anything on his mind?"

"I don't know that I have ever heard a clarinet played with a guilty conscience. I don't know that I would recognise it if I did."

She was, he thought, totally without humour, which made her situation pitiable enough : so he restrained himself and only said gently, "Jude thinks that he has done his best in a difficult situation; it is not altogether his fault that his best was so bad for Daniel. Here comes Janet. Now we shall hear what Matthew thinks."

Janet came back into her room humming under her breath, as if she had forgotten that the two young people were there; but of course there was no need for them to spring apart, they were parted already. Janet noticed this, and put it away with some of her impressions that were much at variance with the general opinions of the school. She had sometimes seen the birth of love between young men and women on their staff; between these two she was sure there was nothing and never would be. Good looks and shared interests, contiguity and mutual esteem were often enough, but not always. She knew that there was a little warmth in Tim's feelings for Tess Pinnegar, which hardly surprised her. Celia she thought rather cold; she had told Matthew so a few weeks after they had appointed her. Matthew had demurred, wondering if her shyness concealed a passionate will and much capacity for growth.

"Matthew says," Janet now said, "to let everything be : as long as there is somebody to sleep with the third form boys he thinks nothing more need be done tonight."

"May I have a word with you, Janet?" Celia now said with a look of supplication to Tim who left them immediately.

"Well, dear?"

She could not say the word; the older woman said it for her.

"You are afraid Daniel may come to some harm, and Jude will be blamed for it." At Celia's speechless nod Janet went on, "I suppose there is a risk, but it is a very slight one. On any other day of the year we should get in touch with the Hardys. We could do so now, they are spending the night at Newcastle Emlyn. But there is nothing they can do, so what is the use of worrying them? He will not fall in the river and drown, it is too shallow; and the chemist's shop will be closed, nobody will sell him enough aspirin to do any harm. I say these things because I know you are thinking them; when they are spoken they sound exaggerated and silly, and that is what they are. Daniel has found some quiet place where he can think things over and decide what he should do. He will be back tomorrow; Matthew is sure of it, and so am I." She added, almost at random, "and so is Jude, or he would not be his usual maddening self." But the effect of these final words surprised her, for Celia turned and ran out of her room as if she were one of the children herself and preferred not to let an adult see her crying.

"The variations I can manage," Owen said when his wife came into their sitting room just after ten o'clock with hot milky drinks and biscuits on a tray. "The second is difficult, and the adagio section; I shall have to ask them to let me take it even slower than usual, or to let me simplify a little. The larghetto is terrible, I mean it is terrible when I play it."

"Stop for a moment now, dear, and have your drink and your

tablets. And I really think we should go to bed early, we must be up by half past six."

Owen put down his violin and took his cup from the tray while Helen watched him, and was happy to see the brightness of his eyes which seemed to contradict what he had said about his difficulties with the quintet.

"Do you think you could play the clarinet part on the piano? And perhaps the viola part with your left hand; it is just a simple rocking bass most of the time, and you could stop playing when it gets harder."

Helen went over to the piano and began to play; what she played sounded beyond belief dreadful. She stopped and looked at the score more carefully.

"The viola part is written in the alto clef," Owen said. "Try the 'cello; that is in the bass. And the clarinet is a transposing instrument. You must play F and C sharp every time, and every note a third lower than it is written."

"What about the B flat, Owen? All the other instruments are playing in D major, and the clarinet part is written in F."

"The clarinet in A plays a G sharp instead of G natural: so if it is to play in D major the G must be flattened. And what looks like B on the score is really G because of playing a third down."

A long silence followed: then Helen tried again, at first uncertainly, but soon with greater confidence as she found that what Owen said was right and that her sight reading was better than she had supposed. At the twentieth bar Owen's fiddle ceased to accompany her lovely tune and began to find work of its own. This was the fifth or sixth time Owen had tried this passage and either increasing familiarity or his wife's presence or even the calming effect of his bedtime drink gave him new strength. The instruments spoke divinely to each other, the violin hushed and yearning, the piano, through whose glittering rhetoric both tried to imagine the limpid eloquence of the woodwind offered if not consolation, at least repose. This was at first rejected; Owen's triplets descending in haste, divided from each other almost by an indrawn breath, anticipated the viola's unappeasable sobbing in the minor variation of the fourth movement. But the clarinet was not beaten, had yet something to say, even in Helen's hands, even in its own absence. Again each hesitant dropping phrase recovered itself, suggesting a renewal of hope; long rising scale passages followed on the violin; sustained single notes floated above them, clear moonlight, full sunshine. The duo ended, the cantilena was repeated. "I cannot make this sing as it should," Helen said sadly, but really there was no need: by now the sweet high notes were as much in their minds as beneath her fingers, and the movement ended in a poignant whisper, too delicate to be called a sigh.

"Shall we try it again?" Owen said a few moments later.

"Yes, if you would like. It is very good, Owen. Jude will be proud of you."

"I cannot manage the proper ornaments," he said in the tone of regret that was natural to him, "and I find those triplets towards the end hard to count; but it is no worse than I thought it would be. I suppose that is because it is music I have known for years; to me it always sounds like a man comforting a woman after the death of their child. That is absurd of course, I can just hear what Jude would say if he heard me lowering Mozart to the status of a composer of film music."

"His own first child died when it was only a few weeks old," Helen said. "But it was not the same thing to lose a child then as now: almost every family must have known something of the kind."

"You think that would have made it easier?" Owen said. "I suppose that you are right. Perhaps it is some help to know that other people have felt what you are feeling and lived through it and managed to be happy again afterwards." Then he thought that she might be taking these words to apply to their present situation which for two hours he had actually forgotten: not even his tablets had reminded him. "When Tess used to have attacks at night," he said, "when she was quite small and we hardly knew how to deal with them, I dreaded that you might have to bear that, and help me bear it. It seems a long time ago, and now she is nearly grown up." He did not say, Tess will help you to bear what is ahead of you; in watching over her future you will eventually find enough happiness to sustain you, since very little will do for a woman of your kind. She understood what he might have said, and why he did not say it, and when they returned to their straitened version of the quintet she gave to each of the clarinet's shimmering cadences its full significance, her chastened heart supplying all that insight Jude's playing could hardly hope to bring to them.

"You are not asleep yet, Tess?"

"No, I do not sleep with my eyes open."

"Can I bring my sleeping bag into your tent? We can talk for a bit, and nobody will be disturbed."

"Janet would not like it: we are on our honour to behave sensibly out here."

"Well, of course, or we should not be sleeping out at all. Just think what might go on, if we were not on our honour."

"I am awfully tired, Kate."

Kate arranged her sleeping bag alongside Tess Pinnegar's, then got into it, then got out again and went back to her own tent. Sleepy voices were raised in protest in the twilight, a boy's voice from the other cluster called out, not too loudly.

"That was Peter," Kate said, getting into her bag, but not lying down.

"Did you hear what he said?"

"Yes, he meant to shock us."

"Suppose I took him at his word?"

Tess began to giggle, Kate giggled too.

"He would run into the house," Tess said, between spasms. "He would go straight to Janet."

"Shall I try it?" Kate gasped, "I mean, really? Just to see what he would do?"

"Oh, not tonight; do let us all get some sleep! Janet is worn out, poor thing. If she and Matthew had to get up and come out here and make us all go inside they would be half-dead in the morning."

"It is all their own fault," Kate said virtuously. "If they were as honest as they set up to be they would let the parents come and see things as they really are, and there would be none of this fuss, just ordinary untidiness and instant coffee and biscuits from a shop and lessons as usual; no concerts, no displays of work, no magazines for sale. Just Cilrheddyn, naked and unashamed."

"The parents would feel let down. They expect a show."

"Yours may; mine are simply glad to come down year after year and find me still here, virgin in mind and body."

"In spite of Peter," Tess said, and the laughter began again and became infectious, became a current of silly gaiety passing between the tents and drawing girls out of some of these to join them.

"Make room in your bag for me, Tess," Nancy begged, and, "Move over Kate. Why is your face so shiny?" a younger girl called Florence asked.

"Cold cream; a woman cannot begin looking after her face too early."

"Can I have some?"

"You are only a little thing, Tess, how is it you take up so much room?"

"I am bony," Tess told Nancy with satisfaction. "My skin is much nearer to my bones than most people's. Jude used to pinch me black and blue when we were little, he said my bruises were much bigger than anyone else's."

"Did he go around pinching other little girls to find out?" Florence said in simple curiosity, as she had no brothers of her own.

"There were Diggory and Tamsin for comparison."

"Jude pinched them, although they are so much smaller?"

"There is no meanness of which the artistic temperament is not capable," Kate said, recovering her cold cream from Florence and passing it on to Nancy, who smelt it for a few moments before silently handing it back.

"This is my last Parents' Day but one," Tess said, as a thought struck her. "I never thought Jude would leave before me."

"We none of us thought he would leave before us," Florence said in a wistful way. "He hasn't even begun to take any notice of girls yet, do you think, Kate?"

"He has taken no notice of me," Kate said, as if this disposed of the question.

"Daniel notices when I do my hair differently. He never says, but I see him looking at it. And Peter does, of course. That is one of the nice things about him."

"What are the others?" Nancy said.

"There is no harm in Peter," Tess said. "He only wants somebody to be kind to him, Kate for preference, but Florence or I would do."

"Or even me," Nancy said.

"You give yourself away, Nancy. You are so cross about sex you will probably turn out to be a nymphomaniac."

"Florence has put her finger on it," Nancy said. "Kate could never have come to that conclusion, never in a million years."

"It is your very last Parents' Day, Nancy."

"Yes, Kate: next year you will have to look after yourself. You will have nobody to guide you except Tess, and Tess is far too kind. You will need to be very sharp with her, Tess, if she is to leave here a pure young maid."

Florence said primly, "I am not at all sure Janet would like us to joke about this."

"Florence is shocked," Nancy said in her calm way. "There is no need. I am just being realistic. Cast an eye on Kate in the moonlight, think of the valley full of wild young Welshmen and you will know that I am right."

"Oh, I thought you meant Peter, or Daniel," Florence said, in open relief.

"What is all this mystery about Daniel?" Nancy said. "Celia came out in a state to fetch Jude, and he went inside and hasn't come out again."

"Poor Daniel," Kate said. "Perhaps I was too hard on him."

"You were too hard on him!" Tess cried in amazement.

"He begged me to give him a photograph, any old photograph I happened to have. He really pleaded, but I was absolutely adamant. I didn't have any, my family only takes colour slides. I could see that he was very upset."

"But all that happened a year ago," Tess said.

"What is a year to a nature like his?"

"Three hundred and sixty-five days," Nancy said. "Now get back to your own tent, Kate, and let us all get some sleep."

"Dark shadows under my eyes improve them, and I prefer to look a little bit pale. I think I shall read for an hour or two, just to make sure."

"Peter has gone to sleep," Florence said in an empty tone when she and Kate stood in the moonlight and no sound came from the boys' tents.

"He needs his rest," Kate said. "The lad is very young."

"She means he has never asked her for a photograph," Nancy said, striding past on fine long legs: she was perfectly right about this.

"Can't you girls be quiet?" a boy's voice now called, a muted voice, but not one to be ignored.

"We are just going to settle down now, Peter," Florence called back.

"Florence is in a little flutter of happiness," Nancy said from the depths of her tent. "The lad is not as young as Kate thought."

"He was calling to us all," Kate said, "and what he said was hardly romantic."

"Then you can get no more satisfaction from it," Nancy told her with severity, "than you allow to Florence."

VI

A SHAFT OF MOONLIGHT fell across Meg's pillow, and she opened unwilling eyes; it seemed as if she had slept only a few minutes, but when she looked at her watch she saw that it was past three. An owl hooted in the woods the other side of the school, her daughter stirred and flopped over; the child's brow shone with moisture, her fringe stuck to it in stiff short wisps. Meg dragged herself out of bed and pulled the blankets off Clare's curled body until only the sheet covered her; she did not wake, although a minute before she had seemed to sleep so lightly. Meg remembered what Celia had said about her never being clumsy with Clare; that young woman's observation, though rarely put into words, was acute. "I am afraid of my child," Meg said now, looking down at the small form with amusement as much for Clare's ready wrath as for her own dread of it. "A temper to go with her hair, as stubborn and self-willed as I was at her age, but at least no scrambling horde of little brothers to tyrannise over, and worship, and wish dead."

This thought led naturally to another : more than a hundred children of all ages, both sexes, every shade of skin, hair and eyes, a wide range of temperament, ability and fortune, were for thirty-six weeks of the year her child's adopted siblings, endlessly seeking out Clare's mother to mend torn clothes, find lost fountain pens, bind up grazed knees. Clare's resentment was open and decided; but she perhaps gained in companionship what she lost in intense communion with her only parent. When the school children went off for the holidays with joy so patent that it was almost a blow in the face for Matthew's love and Janet's patience Clare wandered about the empty spaces, diminished by the absence of those others as she never was by their presence, even in a hundred different shapes all larger than her own. Only the fact that the village school which she attended had longer terms than Cilrheddyn and saw to it that she was never there when

65

the busloads of children actually left at Christmas or Easter or for the long summer holiday preserved them all from terrible scenes; and on the day when they came back she could not come home quickly enough, her own school day lasted a week at least. Then, without a word for her mother, or at best only an impatient "Where's Tess? Is Valerie back?" this least solitary of only children ran off to establish her place in a family enormous, diverse, collectively tolerant and tender.

"Who would have thought," Meg now began to think, as she went back to her bed and stripped off her own blankets; but conjecture was stilled by her sudden awareness that something was happening along the corridor. A sound that was none of the usual ones, the owl, a lavatory flushing, a tap left to drip, a new and persistent sound compelled her attention and soon her active interference. She slipped a dressing gown over her nightdress and left her room. The door of the third form boys' dormitory was closed; scuffling, whimpering, and something not unlike the growls of a dog came from behind it. Meg opened the door with a decisive sweep of her arm and closed her eyes in face of the vivid light that struck them. She had no time thoroughly to take in a confused picture in which Diggory's furious face and another boy's no less furious but tearful as well were the only elements to detach themselves from a general instantaneous impression of rank disorder.

These boys now scrambled for their beds, as did four more, who had been more or less spectators. One bed was left empty, though dishevelled.

"Where is Jude?" Meg said, cutting to the heart of the matter with the ruthlessness that frightened Celia and delighted Diggory who was, as a rule, just such another. At present he felt himself at a disadvantage and did not look at Meg. The boy whose head he had been thumping on the floorboards was also silent, though not with a good will.

"Will somebody tell me what has been happening?" Meg said now, mildly enough.

"Sam had a nightmare," one of the others suggested.

"And Diggory was helping him to get over it?"

"You should not be sarcastic with us, Meg. Janet does not like it."

"Janet does not like fights in the dormitory either," Meg said tartly. "Well, Sam?"

"I had a nightmare."

"And called out?"

"No, I went over to Daniel's bed. Then I remembered it would be Jude so I thought I would go back to sleep again. Then I saw it was nobody, there was nobody there at all."

"And he began to cry," Diggory said. "So then I woke up. I said he could come into my bed : he said that wasn't the same and he was going to tell you."

"And then Diggory thumped me."

The audience of four agreed that this was so, and seemed to think it reasonable.

"Where is Jude?" Meg asked, for the second time.

"I expect he has gone back to his tent."

"Then I shall fetch him. I am going to turn the light out now, Sam, but I will leave the door open; and you are all to keep quiet or you will wake Clare."

The children subsided, agreeing without words that this would be undesirable. Meg went downstairs, took a pair of wellington boots from the cloakroom, and slipped out of the side door, making for the cluster of tents further from the house. She was not sure which was Jude's tent but selected the smallest and least showy as the most likely in view of the Pinnegar's circumstances. At the opening she stooped down and called very softly. Jude's answer was so prompt that she could not think that he had been asleep.

"You must come back to the house, Jude. I shall have to tell Matthew about this."

"I couldn't sleep, all those kids snore. One of them was tossing about and moaning. I suppose he was having a nightmare."

"He was," Meg said coldly. "It woke him, and he looked for comfort. He got Diggory."

"Poor little bastard," Jude said, by way of experiment, but Meg's response was disappointing.

"Diggory, you mean, or Sam Trousdell? I am sorrier for Diggory, I think his loyalty is misplaced. You can look after yourself pretty well, Jude Pinnegar."

"I couldn't sleep," he repeated on a note of sullen incomprehension.

"Then the sooner you get back to bed the better. We all want to see you do yourself justice tomorrow."

"What have you got against me, Meg?"

"Nothing. What should I have? I don't like you much, not at the moment. You see, I am not a bit musical, so I cannot tell myself that everything mean and selfish you do is justified by the pleasure you give me."

Their eyes met; Jude's dropped. He said in a muffled voice, "Daniel was in my tent when I came out."

"Where is he now?"

"He went off as soon as he saw me. I would have let him stay, he could have had my bag, and I don't want a pillow. He can't be far away, it was only a few minutes ago."

"He might sleep in one of the outbuildings," Meg said half to herself, looking away from the orchard to an empty run of stables, almost in ruins, washed to brilliance by the moonlight.

"Anyway," Jude said, with an effect almost of complacence, "he hasn't done himself in, or even run away properly. I knew it couldn't be as bad as everyone made out."

"Then since your conscience is quite at rest you should find it easier to get to sleep," Meg said. He could not miss her anger and his cheeks darkened as he turned away and walked heavily back to the house. Meg sighed, and moved to follow him. A sound, a very slight sound, drew her attention to the other group of tents where the girls slept. She thought for a moment, then slipped quietly over the damp grass. When she stopped she could hear voices whispering. It was impossible to guess whether two girls were together, which happened from time to time, or whether Daniel had taken refuge with Tess. She considered Daniel, she considered Tess; then she went back to the house and got into her cool bed with thankfulness. Clare had not woken. The third form dormitory was silent. The moon slid behind a cloud.

"I will go away while the moon is hidden, Tess."

"Has Meg gone?"

"Yes, I saw the door close behind her. Thank you for hiding me."

"You needn't go if you don't want to. I have enough blankets for two, it is so warm. We could share a pillow."

68

"Lovely Tess. Sweet, sweet Tess. Jude has known you all his life, and thinks you are just a girl, his sister."

"I am a girl and Jude's sister."

"I must go; it will be getting light quite soon."

"Where shall you sleep?"

"I thought of Cilrheddyn church. The key is hung in the porch, I could stretch out on a pew."

"The pews are very hard. Jude and I used to sneak in to play the organ the first year he was here. The place is full of fieldmice. Daniel, there might be bats."

"I am not scared of bats."

"Why wouldn't you stay with Jude if he asked you? Then you could have been friends again and played tomorrow."

"We never have been friends and there is no question of my playing tomorrow."

"Not for Matthew's sake, because Tim says he will be disappointed?"

"Why should Tim want me to ruin his playing, and yours and Jude's and Ian's?"

"You don't ruin it. You only slow us down a little in the variations."

"Look me in the face and say that."

Tess looked him in the face and repeated her words; then Daniel bent down and kissed her. The kiss was full of love but empty of experience, so that Tess accepted it with a bound of delight that was entirely fearless.

"Will you play now?" she said at once, as if this were the natural consequence of his action and her acceptance; her father was, for once in her life, quite forgotten.

"I don't know. No. I will go away and think. Come down to the churchyard after lunch tomorrow, or send Diggory, while the parents are listening to Matthew's speech."

"Daniel!" she cried, sitting bolt upright now in fresh distress. "Your parents! You will have to come back in the morning, they will be worried to death."

"No, they won't. They will be looking at everything, making notes, wondering what they can use."

"Use?"

"For their show. They call it gathering material."

"You mean, you came to Cilrheddyn to help them get ideas for their writing?" Tess said, her eyes huge with wonder.

"I expect so," Daniel said grimly. "Can you think of any better reason? I haven't got asthma, I am not specially gifted or maladjusted or anything, and while Dinah goes on working I could still be at home because my grandmother is there, my own mother's mother. She would look after me, she did that before my father married Dinah."

Tess could not sort so much out at three o'clock in the morning. She shook her head as if aware of some discrepancy in Daniel's recital; she was not quite convinced.

"They would not get much material, visiting you half a dozen times a year."

"There are my letters. I write long ones."

"Do you? Jude and I bring back a dozen postcards each term with stamps on, and send one off each week. They really only want to be sure we are still alive."

"Gran likes me to write about everything. There isn't always much, but I spin it out."

"Do you think you will be a writer one day? I mean, you might have inherited it, like Jude and I from Daddy, only ours is music."

"Everybody wants to write who can't do anything else."

She missed his bitterness and said eagerly, "You are really clever, Daniel, there are lots of things you could do: but why not write, if you enjoy it?"

"What is there to write about? What do I know? Nothing has ever happened to me."

"You could make things up, and fill in with places you have been to. You hitch-hiked to Italy, you must have got some material there."

"Of a kind."

"You wouldn't need much," she said, kneeling now on her pillow in the warm, the newly stirring dawn. "Your parents don't seem to need an awful lot for their thing."

"Hackwork," he said, with dreadful scorn.

"I expect they make quite a bit of money," Tess suggested.

"I don't want to write for money. It is sickening to hear them talk about what the public wants."

"Yes, I expect so, sickening," she said, her lids drooping.

"If I write I would like it to be because I felt I must, I had to : you know, as if it were the only thing worth doing."

"Yes, of course," she said, beginning to rock slightly on her knees.

"But I don't really feel strongly about it yet."

"Couldn't you," Tess said, with a tremendous effort, "talk it over with your father? Ask his advice?"

"What would he know about it?"

"He probably didn't think about what the public wanted either, when he was younger. But now, with you and your stepmother and your grandmother to think of . . ."

Her voice trailed off, she smiled fatuously, and slid down on to her pillow.

"Domesticity," Daniel said, "has been the ruin of many a fine artist."

She did not hear him, nor would she have assented to this proposition if she had, instancing various lives, to which he would have opposed as many others. Leaving her, none the less, in the faint but augmenting light was sufficiently hard to cause this boy the faintest premonitory pang; the very earliest knowledge of his own, gleaned not from books or hearsay, of how irreconcilable are those claims, how discordant the voices of self-regard and love.

By four o'clock sufficient light was filtering through the flowered chintz curtains of her bedroom to wake Muriel Daintry; she seldom slept past four nowadays, even in winter. "Sometimes I go off again for a little while, round about seven," she told her son-in-law's wife if Dinah found her sleeping when she came in with the breakfast tray, "but very few people could manage with as little rest as I do." "Yes, you are wonderfully fresh in the evenings," Dinah said on these occasions, "when Vincent and I are absolutely worn out. You put us both to shame." Neither of them mentioned what both of them well knew; those afternoon hours consecrated to letter writing or the perusal of magazines, but spent as often as not in gentle and rewarding slumber. Since letters had to be written, and magazines presumably to be read, Muriel went to bed with all she needed close at hand; even at a hotel she made sure she would not be left unoccupied, and sat up now to finish a story she had started to read on the journey down. Her daughter, Daniel's mother, had laughed at her outright for her choice of reading: Vincent regularly, once a week at least, picked up the current novel, read a few sentences aloud in a voice of scorn, and wondered, also aloud, how she could waste her time on such rubbish. She had never minded her daughter's ridicule or Vincent's scorn, but she did not like Dinah's indulgence; for such indulgence seemed to imply that it did not matter how she wasted her time, since she had nothing better to do.

At five she got out of bed, put on her dressing gown and went along the passage to the lavatory; the door was not locked, she went in. The little boy she had seen in the dining room the night before was standing with his back to her in his pyjamas. Before she could go away he turned round. He was not much embarrassed.

"You should lock the door," Mrs. Daintry said, with quiet severity. "I have had a little boy to look after, so I do not mind. But some ladies would think it very rude of you."

"I thought I might not be able to get it open again. Then I should have to shout, and people wouldn't like that so early in the morning."

"That was sensible," Mrs. Daintry said. "Now may I come in, please, and will you go away?"

"Should I pull the chain, or will you do it for both of us, so as not to make a noise twice?"

"I will do it for both of us."

Robert left her alone, but when she came out of the lavatory he was standing in the passage looking helplessly first one way and then the other.

"What is it now? Can't you find your way back to your room? How old are you?"

"Nine, nearly ten."

"When my grandson was your age he could look after himself very well. I like a boy to be able to stand on his own feet."

Robert was to his certain knowledge doing exactly this, but he looked down nevertheless, to make sure. Mrs. Daintry's rosy cheeks grew even rosier.

"You should not be impertinent, especially to a lady, especially to an elderly lady whom you do not know." The child was silent; experience had taught him the risks of explanation. He also

72

judged, correctly, that this elderly lady, though fiercer than her looks suggested, would probably, at a pinch, help him to regain his room.

"Do you remember the number on the door?" she asked now, with severity only a fraction diminished.

"I think it was eight. Or it might have been eleven."

"Concentrate!" Muriel said, and the child drew his brows together, this change in his expression bearing no relation whatever to the processes of his mind, which had ground to a halt in the clear realisation that he had no idea that his bedroom door had had a number on it at all. Muriel clucked and moved off along the passage, Robert hurried in her wake.

"I think I left the door open. I am almost sure I did."

"Well, that is something. Here is my room, number twenty-one. If yours is eight or eleven it will not be on this floor. Did you come up a flight of stairs, do you think?"

"I think I would remember stairs."

"I don't think you would remember your head if it were not fixed on to your shoulders," Muriel said, but extended a hand as much in exasperation as in kindness. "You had better come with me until the maid brings my tea. Then she can find out where your room is."

Robert followed her into her room and looked about him.

"Have you lived here a long time?"

"Of course not. Why should you think that?"

"There are so many things here that don't look as if they belong to the hotel, and not just clothes."

"I like to make any place I stay in reflect a little of my personality," Muriel said. "Are you hungry? There are biscuits in that tin."

He took a ginger nut, then seated himself not without trepidation on a hard chair by the window.

"I shall get back into bed," Muriel said. "I have a long day ahead of me."

"It is the same number of hours as all the days," Robert said.

"No, it is not, because it has begun so early, and because I am getting on in years."

"When my mother says I have a long day ahead of me she means because I am young and will be up late."

"There you are then," Muriel said, and hung her dressing

gown tidily upon the back of the door. "There is a magazine there if you would like to look at it."

"No, thank you."

"Are you cold?"

Robert shook his head, but without conviction.

"You may get under my eiderdown if you like. There, I will put the pillows straight. Perhaps you can sleep a little. I shall read. It is only just after five, and you will need more rest."

She opened her book, allowing Robert a generous share of the bed. For a little while the novelty of his situation kept him awake, but the miseries of the night before had depleted him. He did just wonder if his mother, finding his bed empty, might suffer a shock; if his father, coming in response to her tearful summons, might know the pangs of remorse. These things were possible, and would lead, as all things did, to wrath and remonstrations. In the meantime Mrs. Daintry's faint flowery scent was delicious in his nostrils, the prettiness of her possessions scattered around the indifferent room spoke of charming ease, of soft conditions to which nothing in this child's life had yet accustomed him. He slept; and some time later Muriel's book slipped from her plump white fingers on to the counterpane and she slept too.

"I expect the Hardys will bring Muriel Daintry with them," Janet had said to her brother when she left him at the end of the long evening of preparation and planning. "She is a tiresome woman and Daniel's disappearance will make her even worse than usual."

With this thought she had gone to bed : with this thought she woke. The lightest of winds ruffled her curtains, insistent birds clamoured in the branches of the tree beneath her window. She got up and dressed, choosing an old suit and stout shoes. Then she went very quietly down the stairs and out of the door Meg had used some hours earlier, crossing between the two groups of tents and making for a path through the narrow strip of woodland that separated the grounds of the school from the road; Nancy saw her go, Nancy who did most of her work before breakfast in order to have the rest of the day to supervise Kate's and Florence's, or so she said. "Shall I be like that when I am over sixty?" was the girl's thought. "Yes, probably. I am no more likely to marry than Janet, and if she were married she

74

would lie still so as not to wake her husband. Kate would get up if she wanted to, and perhaps Florence would, unless she marries Peter, but Tess would never stir."

Janet opened a wicket gate and came out on the road, walked uphill for a hundred yards and then turned right between high hedgerows, plunging downhill on a lane which soon became a track, dusty at first, muddy further down. Ruined buildings, a barn, two or three cottages in a row were on her left; there was not a pane of glass in any of the windows. Nettles grew as high as her breast in the abandoned gardens, the low grey walls were starred with hart's-tongue and smeared with the gleaming tracks of snails. Beyond the cottages under blackthorn and elder the track bent to the right and came to an end. Janet opened another wicket gate and came into the churchyard.

It was full of graves, and the graves, it was to be supposed, were full of people. Of the visitation of the living the place showed at first no sign. There were nettles here too and rich offerings of convolvulus twined about the neglected headstones. By one of these Janet paused, arrested by some slight difference; the size of the grave perhaps, as it was a child's, or the presence among the creamy bells of the bindweed of blooms of a different shape and hue, two or three wilted heads of honeysuckle. She looked more closely and saw that these were not growing, but had been plucked and laid carelessly upon the grave, if such a gesture could be made without care. Then she read the inscription on the headstone, and went into the porch of the church, where a notice was pinned up announcing that a service would be held there the second Sunday of every month. "Next week," Janet said to herself: strange as it seemed, the jungle growth behind her was only three weeks old. A week from now, as on the second Saturday in June, half a dozen men and women would appear with scythes and secateurs, dusters and mops. Order would be brought to the church and its graveyard, official flowers in vases would adorn the graves, but not the one that was already decked, for who recalled that boy, more than a hundred years dead? Who, except perhaps Daniel?—whom Janet now saw as she pushed open the heavy door with a controlled hand. She saw only the top of his head, where he rested it against the back of a pew. He did not move; she could not tell if she had woken him, but this was of no importance, he was safe, he was not far away. She

75

closed the door as soundlessly as she had opened it and went back to the school.

"Daniel is all right," she said to Jude, passing him on the stairs with swimming things under his arm. "I think Jude was relieved to hear that Daniel is safe and sound," she told Meg outside Meg's door, but Meg knew better. "What's wrong with Clare?"

"She wants to put her new dress on now, and I say no, she is to wear a shirt and jeans until breakfast is over, in case she spills and spoils it."

"You are in shirt and jeans yourself: doesn't that make her see how right you are?"

"No, it only makes her determined to prove me wrong," Meg said, and raised her voice. "Get dressed and come down to breakfast, Clare. If you go on making that noise I shall put the dress away for the rest of the day."

Meg's threats, like Nancy's, were never idle, and Clare knew this and ceased to howl. Soon she came downstairs and into the dining room, seating herself with the youngest children and pouring cornflakes into a bowl. Tess presided over this table, and saw to it that not too much milk was squandered on the cloth.

"Daniel is all right," Clare told her. "I heard Janet tell my mother."

"How did Janet know?"

"I don't think she said. They were talking about me, it was just the one thing about Daniel."

"Why should anyone talk about you?" said the girl who sat next to her. "You are not important."

"I am important to my mother."

"Well, of course."

"She wanted me to wear my new frock, but I said no, I had better wear something old down to breakfast in case I had an accident."

"That was very sensible of you, Clare," Tess said kindly, with a little frown for the other child. "Valerie, won't that knitted dress be rather hot on such a warm day?"

"Meg thought it might," Valerie said, "but I don't feel the heat as much as other people."

"And it is very short," Clare said, "your knees stick out so far they will help to cool you down."

76

> "Valerie's knees
> Will wave in the breeze,"

Diggory said, collecting empty cereal bowls as it was his turn to
wait at this table. "Does everybody want greasy bacon and raw
sausage?"

"Diggory!" Tess cried in reproof, but he had gone and
Valerie's disposition to weep had asserted itself.

"Would you like my handkerchief?" Clare asked with interest.
"I don't suppose there is any room in that dress for a pocket."

"It is wonderful that Valerie could knit a dress at all at her
age," Tess said desperately. "You are a very clever girl, Valerie.
I wish I could knit as well as you."

But Valerie left the table, narrowly avoiding a collision with
Diggory.

"Don't you want your cooked breakfast?"

"No."

"She would choke," Clare said, and this did indeed seem
likely. "I will have her sausage."

"No, you won't," Diggory said. "I will: waiter's perks. And
you don't deserve an extra sausage, you are a spiteful child. I
shall tell my sister Tamsin to pull your hair hard."

"That is enough, Diggory. Tamsin need not be spiteful just
because Clare is."

"Am I spiteful?" Clare asked, as if there might just be a
doubt.

"No more than I was at your age," Tess said; but this was
quite untrue, and all of them knew it and loved her for the lie.

"Shall we stop, Owen, and have breakfast? There is that nice
field with the gorse bushes and harebells and the lovely view."

"I shall be carsick if we don't have something soon," Tamsin
said, and Owen immediately drew in to the side of the road and
stopped the car. It was barely eight o'clock but the sky was
already bleached, the first freshness had dried off the grass.

"It is going to be very hot," Helen said, pouring coffee.

"I brought my swimming things," Tamsin said. "Lucky Jude!
He will be in the water already. I wish we had a swimming pool
in the garden and I could go in before breakfast every morning."

"Jude only does it so as to get out of having a proper bath at night," Helen said, for her adoration for her son did not entirely blind her. While Tamsin wandered off to look for rabbits she said quickly to Owen, "How are you, dear? I hope you are not worn out after all that practice last night."

"Not a bit," he said stoutly, "and the roads are far less crowded than I expected."

But the thought of the heat and the hours of driving ahead dismayed him, and the confidence he had felt the evening before in his own drawing room playing to his wife had not survived a night of pitiless dreams in which the strings of his fiddle continually snapped or his music fell to pieces. On Jude's square face the momentary derisive grin he knew so well grew rigid, Tess passed her father more music, another violin, but a mouse crept out of it to run up his sleeve and nestle finally under his chin. He could not play without disturbing it, but the audience and even Jude began to laugh at his predicament, and Owen laughed too, since there was nothing else to be done, and woke laughing, which Helen took to be a good omen for the day.

"You will be able to play with the little Lindsay girl while Daddy and I are at the parents' meeting after lunch," Helen now said to Tamsin, and gave her a cup of milk and an egg sandwich.

"I don't like Clare: I would rather be with Diggory."

"Diggory will be having lunch with us," her mother said, with a clear memory of her second son's icy dislike of Tamsin's attention on public occasions. "He will want to be off with his friends in the afternoon."

"He has his friends all the time. He hasn't seen me since Sports Day."

"Perhaps he will have a swim with you," Owen said, continuing in the optimistic vein that seemed to soothe his wife.

"If he does it will be the first time," Tamsin said. "He doesn't swim as well as I do."

"Don't be difficult, dear," her mother said, with a slight frown.

"I shall ask Tess to look after me."

"Tess may need to help Daddy rehearse."

"How can she if he is at the parents' meeting?" Tamsin said in a sweetly reasonable tone.

"Suppose we leave all the plans until we get there," Owen said, finishing his coffee with a sense of storm impending.

"Yes, of course," Helen said at once. "There is no need to decide anything now. The important thing is for everyone to have a lovely day. Drink up your milk, Tamsin, and try to sleep the rest of the way, then you will be in a good temper when you wake up, ready to enjoy everything."

Daniel awoke with a start: a mouse had run up his arm, its whiskers brushed against his neck. For a moment he could not grasp what had happened, and thought it was a spider or something else offensive and cold-blooded. He dashed the back of his hand against his throat and the little animal was knocked on to the pew beside him. He put out a hand to pick it up, but it whisked out of his reach and down to the floor faster almost than his glance could follow. He was glad his thoughtless movement had not injured it, and somehow pleased that his sleeping self had seemed so little of a menace. His joints ached, his back was stiff, he was above all hungry. He looked for the bag of crisps he had brought for his breakfast and saw that it was this and not his warmth and stillness that had attracted the mouse: a corner of the bag had been nibbled away, and crumbs lay mixed with droppings on the seat. A slight revulsion was soon overcome, he picked up the bag and went out into the sunlit churchyard. By the time the crisps were finished his hunger had given way to thirst. There was a tap in the vestry, and some jamjars, meant to serve as vases for the graves. He drank out of one of these; the water was brackish and tepid.

The long morning, the whole day stretched out in front of him. He had no idea what he would do. A plan he had conjured up overnight seemed in the daytime full of imperfections. He had thought of strolling back to the school, seizing the proper moment, and hiding in his father's car. Then on the drive back to London and when the first shock was over and he had offered some sort of explanation they would simply take him home. With every moment that passed he saw more objections to this simple stratagem: would Vincent and Dinah for instance simply stay at Cilrheddyn all day if he were not there? Wouldn't they rather turn round and head straight for home in case he had really run away, and taken the train from Cardigan? And if they did stay, could he count on remaining undiscovered until the afternoon, perhaps late afternoon, or even early evening? What should he do for lunch, after so frugal a breakfast? And how would Tess feel when she came to the churchyard and found him gone?

He sat down finally, with no decisions made, on the child's grave he had cleared the evening before, tossing the wilted honeysuckle angrily into the long grass. But a few moments later he got up and went to the vestry, where he filled a jamjar with water and carried it back to the grave. He went in search of flowers and when he had found enough he put them in the jar and set it down where the headstone offered a little shade from the sunlight, already intense, though it was not yet nine o'clock. Then he sat on the steps of the church and took a book out of his pocket. He could not imagine what else there might be to do.

VII

"THERE OUGHT TO be an amnesty for breakages on Parents' Day," the sturdy brown-haired boy called Peter said, picking up the pieces of a cup that Diggory had dropped and looking around for somewhere to put them, "but since there isn't, chalk up your score on the board and be more careful with the next tray."

The Spaniards stood in a row under the long kitchen window; one scraping dishes, the next washing, the next rinsing, the last drying. Peter's job was to see that the second and third formers delivered the dirty things to José and took the clean ones from Serafina with reasonable dispatch. Between one batch of Spaniards or Italians or Cypriots, for they tended to come and go in batches like migratory birds, the pupils took over the dishwashing. They did it with constant complaint, telling any member of the staff within earshot that this was not what their parents paid for. "You would not like to eat off unwashed plates," Meg said. "I wouldn't mind, as long as it was the same plate," Peter, or it might have been Florence or Daniel said. "Try it for a day or two, and see how you get on. Write a label and make sure you get the right plate for every meal." Nobody accepted her challenge and Meg continued to make out lists and rotas for laying the tables and sweeping the dining room; she was privately thankful when there was a full complement of domestic staff, but nobody except Janet ever guessed this.

"The children say Daniel is back," Celia said to Peter when he came out of the pantry. "Do you know if that is true?"

"He was back for a while during the night," Peter said. "I think he has gone off again."

"Back during the night, whatever do you mean?"

"I don't think I should say any more," Peter said with an air of satisfaction as he saw the colour come into her cheeks. "I couldn't say any more, without seeming to slander a young lady we both know."

"Was it Daniel who was in Tess Pinnegar's tent, then?" Meg said, handing him a forgotten tray at the dining room door. "I am glad it was Daniel, and not you."

"What did she mean by that?" Peter said with the smirk of one who knows very well what is meant.

"I think she meant that we all trust Daniel," Celia said. "We all know he is thoroughly sensible."

"What a thing to know about anybody!" Peter said. "I am glad nobody even suspects that of me."

"You should not pretend to be worse than you are, Peter. It is such a silly pose."

"I thought it would be less silly than pretending to be better. At least, less ordinary."

"What are you supposed to be doing now?" Celia said, with an effect of putting many years between them; an effect Meg's caustic speeches seldom had, though she was considerably older than Celia.

"Putting up signs to the numerous attractions we have to offer. What are you supposed to be doing now, Celia?"

"I shall find Nancy and help her to arrange the sale of work," Celia said, with all the dignity that she could muster, but it was not enough; the boy was laughing at her and she could not join in the laughter, her dignity was too precious to her, though there was not nearly enough of it for protection. She went out to the courtyard where the shadows were almost intense enough to make the Spaniards feel at home.

"Celia is upset again," Nancy said. "What little steps she takes!"

"She is afraid her heels will catch in the cobbles," Kate said. "Anyone might worry about that."

"But nobody does, except Celia. We have just finished, Celia: but we have left the cakes and strawberries in the Domestic Science room in case flies get on them."

"It looks very nice," Celia said. "I think that notice ought to be given a little more prominence, Kate. The parents will like to know what a good cause they are giving their money to."

"In case they thought they were just buying our cakes and pots and cheeseboards," Nancy said. "That would seem like extravagance."

Kate moved a notice, nicely lettered, which said that the proceeds of the sale were to be devoted to famine relief.

"Do you think that oblong dish is worth five shillings, Nancy? The glaze is so uneven."

"It is like big drops of cold gravy," Nancy said, with a glance at the dish in question. "It is a very large dish, a joint of meat could go on it, if it were a little joint, and then the glaze would go unnoticed. A big dish, imitation gravy, and the satisfaction of having contributed to a good cause : five shillings is cheap for all that."

"But at that rate," Celia said, "there is nothing to stop us charging anything we like for all our little efforts."

"Nothing does stop us," Nancy said, "except a knowledge of the circumstances of our parents."

"Have you room for the school magazines?" Peter said, coming up with a sheaf of these under his arm, "or should I bring out another table?"

"We can manage," Kate said with a brilliant smile. "I will just shift that dish a little."

"Celia's conscience will be easier now," Nancy said, picking up what remained of the dish from the cobbles. "How all things work together for them that love God!"

"Do you think I should put five shillings in the tin?" Kate said.

"What do you think?"

"I only have fifteen shillings left of my pocket money, and there are still three weeks of term."

"Children are starving all over Africa and India," Nancy said, her stern tone only partly assumed.

"Do you think any parent would have bought that dish, if I had not broken it?" Kate said to Peter.

"My parents wouldn't. There isn't a flat surface anywhere at home that hasn't at least three bits of my awful pottery on it."

"Should you think," she now besought him, "half a crown would be fair?"

"I can see it will have to be," Nancy said. "Put those magazines down, Peter, and find something useful to do before Kate smashes anything else."

"I have finished here, I mean Nancy can manage well enough without me, at least until people start to buy things. Shall I come and help you, Peter?"

"Yes, do that," Nancy said. "Make sure there is a notice

outside the back door, Peter, pointing this way. I don't want to sit here alone all day with just a half crown in the tin."

"If nobody else wants it, Nancy," Celia said in a tone that was meant to be easy, "I should like that green mug, the one with the wheatear design."

"Shall I put it away for you?"

"No, not now. It seems wrong to take our choice before any of the parents has even looked to see what is specially nice."

"I will hide it behind Florence's jar. But I don't think it is specially nice. Ian has done some much better things, that jug, for instance."

"Did Ian make the mug?" Celia said, less easily.

Nancy picked the mug up and looked at its underside.

"Yes, here are his initials, I.D."

"I thought the I was a J," Celia said, "And there is a sort of tail on the D."

"Yes, it is messy. But Ian certainly made this one, I remember him giving it to me."

"Now I come to look at it more closely I don't think so much of it. You need not try to keep it for me. How much are the magazines this year?"

"Two shillings."

"I will take one now, then you will have a coin to rattle in each of your tins."

Nancy gave her a magazine and Celia wandered off to join Tim.

"I thought you would be in the music room."

"I don't want the children to get stale. There is nothing more we can do until Mr. Pinnegar gets here."

"Is Jude thrilled at the thought of playing with his father?"

"Not thrilled; resigned. He is a hard boy to please. I like your dress, Celia. That fresh green suits you."

She coloured up as Florence might have done, and Kate and Florence saw this and exchanged meaning glances as they stood by Peter in one of the passageways.

"Only one more notice," Peter said, climbing down the set of steps.

"Oh, be careful, the bottom rung is all lopsided!" Florence cried, but too late.

84

"You might have told me sooner," he said from the floor, white-faced.

"She may have thought you would have noticed on the way up," Kate said.

"Why, Nancy might have said that!" Florence cried. "You are not usually so unkind."

"Could one of you help me up?" Peter said, and winced as both the girls did this.

"What is it?"

"Have you broken something, do you think?"

"Kate, shouldn't we fetch Meg or Janet?"

"Yes, you should. I will stay with him."

"Why, we are not in the outback!" Florence said with indignation. "He will be safe enough if he just waits here."

"I don't want Meg or Janet," Peter said between his teeth, "and I haven't broken anything, I have only grazed my knee."

"A handkerchief—" Kate said, producing one, flowered, with lace.

"What a useless little thing!" Florence remarked.

"Have you a better?"

"No, I don't seem to have one at all."

"Then unless you want to rip your dress up you need not be rude about mine."

"Rip my dress up, what an idea! I don't know where you get such ideas, Kate."

"From me, by telepathy," Peter said, lolling more or less at ease against the wall and accepting their quarrel as a tribute, in much the same spirit that he had accepted Kate's handkerchief.

Florence walked away, her dusky head bowed.

"That was not very nice of you, Peter. The child adores you."

"That is not very nice of you, Kate. If you have any reason to think the child adores me you should keep it to yourself."

"I suppose you think we all worship you," she said, tossing her harvest hair.

"Nancy doesn't, Tess doesn't. And Celia prefers Jude."

"Oh, Peter! She is old enough to be his mother; or no, she is not. But an aunt, or an older sister."

"I read a book once about a young boy who was initiated by an older woman, in France."

"Oh well, in France."

"They say two virgins together is a mistake. Somebody has to know something, or it may be a flop."

"Flopping together might not be so bad. May I have my handkerchief back now, if your knee has stopped bleeding?"

"I would like to keep it, in memory of a very beautiful occasion."

"It is the only one I have," Kate said.

"You are supposed to bring twelve back at the beginning of term."

"I bring paper ones, in case of a cold. And this one for special occasions."

"You cannot use it any more today. It has blood all over it."

"I could say my nose bled."

"Let me keep it, Kate."

She gave it to him, and he screwed it up into a ball and put it in the pocket of his khaki shorts.

"Are you going to change?"

"God, yes. You don't think I'd let my parents see me like this!"

"Then don't forget to take my handkerchief out of your pocket. If it goes to the laundry I shall get it back. It has my nametape in the corner."

"That is just as well," Peter said, leaving her. "Otherwise I might forget whose handkerchief it was, as the years go by."

"The magazine seems to change very little from year to year."

"The names change under the poems."

"This year they are all anonymous," Celia said. "It is so silly, when everybody knows who wrote them."

"Speak for yourself," Meg said; she had come into the staff common room with a handful of letters, and stayed to sit down with a cigarette.

"Well, this one about suddenly finding out that life isn't worth living; that must be Upper Fifth or Sixth form, and probably a girl."

Meg took Celia's magazine and read the poem.

"Yes; Florence, do you think?"

"Not Tess or Nancy, and Kate would never have heard of accidie. So Florence."

"What about this one, the elegy?"

"Harder to say, because it is so impersonal. But since it is for D. H. Lawrence, a boy: perhaps Daniel."

"Why a boy? Why not Kate? She brought 'Lady Chatterley' back with her, it was right on top of her trunk where she knew I would see it unpacking."

"What did you say?"

"Nothing. She was very disappointed."

"Kate couldn't write a poem, not even this one without any long words. And girls may read Lawrence but they don't always like him, he makes it so hard for a woman to do right."

"It is quite a good poem, I think," Meg said. "Of course I am no judge.

'He shall not be raised at the bright blast
Of trumpets, nor shall the ruined saints
Shatter his distances of rest
With reconciliation and promises
Of their eternity where no peace is.' "

" 'Distances of rest' is weak," Celia said, "and rest isn't the first thought that Lawrence brings to mind. It is a very young poem."

"As it would be, in a school magazine."

"Yes, one must judge with charity."

"It seems odd for me to be giving you a lesson in charity," Meg said, with her rare laugh. "You are a much kinder person than I am, Celia."

"Only a more timid one, really," Celia said.

"Did you write this, Florence, this 'Elegiac Sonnet'?"

"Let me see, Tess," Diggory said, trying to pull the magazine out of his sister's hands.

"Buy one yourself. You must have some pocket money left."

"I broke a cup this morning, and Peter saw me, so I shall have to pay for it."

"If I lend you five shillings will you let me have it back at the beginning of the holidays?"

"With interest?"

"No, of course not."

"You need not bite my head off," Diggory said in an injured tone. "I am only trying to teach you to manage your affairs in a sensible way."

"If I were sensible I would lend you nothing, and I would not let you look at my magazine."

"It is about Lawrence," Diggory cried, looking at it with delight, "Florence, Florence, wrote a poem about Lawrence."

"I hope there are none of your awful verses in there," Tess said. "Forgive him, Florence, he is only a little boy."

"If you hadn't asked me, he would never have thought I might have written it," Florence said coldly.

"He doesn't know now, he only thinks he does."

"Florence never said she didn't," Diggory said. "She can't have written all the anon ones, though, not with seven O-levels to get through. And I know she didn't, because there is a whole page of mine at the end, Tess."

Tess snatched the magazine back and turned to the last page.

"Diggory, what a little beast you are! How could you, those stupid rhymes!"

"The editor thought they were clever," Diggory said with complacency.

"Oh, Peter! Jude will be furious, he will beat you up, and you deserve it."

"I only put J and three spaces for him, and T and three spaces for you, so as not to be libellous."

"So many names begin with J and rhyme with rude, or with T and rhyme with mess," Florence said.

"I am better at rhymes than you are: there isn't a proper rhyme in the whole of your sonnet."

"Look!" Tess cried, "there is a car, the first parents have arrived!"

"They are very early," Florence said, transferring some of her indignation from Diggory to the Branksomes.

"Who are they, Diggory?" Tess said. "Do you know?"

"They are not real parents," Diggory said, "they are only prospective customers. You had better be on your best behaviour, Florence."

Florence smacked his leg, hard, and he chased her round the courtyard with fierce cries. Emma got out of the car and Robert stood by her, clutching her hand so hard that it hurt.

"I suppose we have come to the right place?" Harry said.

"Perhaps we should ask that nice girl with the long hair."

"I would rather go to the sea," Robert said. "I would like to go now."

"Later, dear, perhaps. We are going to see Miss Storace and her brother."

"I don't want to see anybody. I don't like this place."

"Oh, for heaven's sake!" Harry cried in disgust. "It is only a boy not much bigger than you chasing a girl. Nobody is going to hurt you, Robert."

"Should we ask them what they want, do you think, Tess?" Florence said. "Pax now, Diggory, I have no breath left."

"Promise not to hit me again ever?"

"I shall hit you whenever you deserve it. I hope you don't mind my hitting your little brother, Tess?"

"It saves me the trouble," Tess said calmly. "What do you suppose is the matter with that little boy?"

"He is afraid of Florence," Diggory said, "and we all know how right he is to be frightened."

"Diggory, go and ask him if he would like to see the rabbits."

"Ask him yourself."

"I don't think he would leave his mother, Tess," Florence said. "Perhaps we should ask them all."

"That man with the eyebrows doesn't look as if he would care for rabbits," Diggory said. "I know, Tess, shall I sell him your magazine, as you have finished looking at it?"

Tess ignored him and went up to Harry and Emma.

"Were you looking for somebody? Can I help you?"

"Miss Storace is expecting us," Emma said with a grateful look. "Actually we are a few minutes early."

"Diggory will find her for you," Tess said, and at a look from her Diggory walked across to the main building, dragging his feet. "Would you like to come and see where the pets live?" she said to Robert, who thrust his face further into Emma's skirts.

"Of course he would," Harry said roughly. "Robert is always asking us for a pet of his own but in a town house we cannot manage."

"We lived in a flat when I was little," Tess said, "and there was room on the balcony for guinea pigs. And there are always budgies and goldfish."

"It is my fault really," Emma said. "Robert is too young to

look after an animal himself, and so we have none. But if you came here, Robert, you could have a rabbit."

"Who would look after it in the holidays?" Harry said.

"Oh, we could think about that when the time came."

"It is not much use raising the child's hopes when they will very likely come to nothing."

Tess looked from Harry's dark face to Emma's fair distressed one with a sense that more was being said and felt than just the words these people spoke. She held out her hand to the child.

"My little sister will be here soon, she is about your age. We always go to the cook for carrot peelings when she comes and take them with us; if you like I will take you to the kitchen now, and then we will be ready for Tamsin."

"Tamsin and Diggory!" Harry said, as she walked away with his son. "What names to give children! What an infliction!"

"They are out of books, Harry, novels of Thomas Hardy's."

"Well, I did not suppose their parents had made them up. It is just as I thought, everything second rate, arty and pretentious."

"But the girl was very nice," Emma said, looking after her son as if she would have liked to join him. "You must admit, Harry, she was very pleasant and unaffected. And see how Robert has taken to her! I thought he would cling to me all the morning."

"He took to her because she treated him with confidence. That is all it takes with young children."

Emma could not say to her husband that his unperturbed confidence seemed not to have been enough on some occasions. She bit her lip, and looked at her shoes.

"Now we shall have to wait here until she chooses to bring our son back," Harry said.

"It gives us time to look round a little. Should we go and see the things on that stall?"

"The mugs and beakers and ashtrays are half a crown each, the flower pots are two shillings, the medium sized vases and dishes are five shillings each and the big ones have the prices on them because they are all different. The money goes to famine relief."

Nancy delivered herself of these words in her light rapid contralto at such a speed that her first customers of the day understood very little except that everything was for sale and nothing was very dear.

"I like those pendants, Harry."

"Shall I buy you one? Which?"

"The blue one with the trefoil design."

"How much?" Harry asked.

"Whatever you like, as long as it is more than three shillings."

"That is an odd way to do business," he said as they walked away and Emma slipped the leather thong that carried the pendant over her head.

"It was not really business, after all. Do you suppose that Robert is all right?"

"The rabbits will not have eaten him. And if he were crying we should hear him, he knows how to make himself heard."

"There is the boy Diggory."

"I can't find Janet," Diggory said. "She could be anywhere, except all the places I looked in. Would you care to buy a school magazine?"

"Oh, yes, thank you. I will pay for it, Harry. How much is it?"

"Well, this one is secondhand. I can let you have it for one and threepence."

"Does the money go to famine relief?"

"Yes," Diggory said, with no sense of telling a lie, since he fully intended to relieve somebody's hunger.

"What should we do, Harry, about looking for Miss Storace?"

"We can sit down here," Harry said, leading the way to a bench, "and when the girl brings Robert back we will ask her. She would know more than her brother."

"Can I get you something to eat?" Florence said, coming out of one of the rooms that opened on to the courtyard and which for this one day in the year was turned into a sort of al fresco restaurant with all its doors pulled back and tables outside on the cobbles.

"Thank you very much, but it seems no time since we had breakfast."

"There is free coffee for the parents in the library at eleven," Florence said regretfully. "We charge for it here: of course it is all in a good cause. The coffee in the library is real, we would not make any profit if ours was."

"These children seem to have a well developed commercial

outlook," Harry said. "There was a great deal in the prospectus about individual fulfilment and community growth, but nothing about buying and selling and girls dressing up as waitresses and touting for orders."

"It cannot do them any harm. Handling money and giving change would be a good practical way of learning arithmetic."

"Yes, for six year olds," Harry said, exploding into indignation.

"Let us not start judging too soon. You must agree that the setting is beautiful; the grey stone and the cobbles, the woods along the road, that old mounting block, the sundial over the gateway."

"It is pleasant enough now, with the sun shining. It would be less so on a wet day, or in winter."

"Yes, of course. But so would any place. I wish that girl would come back, it is ten o'clock now and Janet will be expecting us."

Because Janet was expecting them she came down to the courtyard and advanced over the cobbles to meet them with her hand held out and a curious tripping gait.

"Emma, dear, how lovely it is to see you!"

"It is such a long time, longer than I care to remember. This is my husband—Harry, this is Janet Storace, I have told you so much about her."

Harry shook hands with Janet who looked up at him with a gaze of full appraisal which gave way to a smile only just in time for so involved an onlooker as his wife.

"I am very pleased to meet you, Professor Branksome. I won't say I have heard so much about you, because we are very much out of the world here, and our children are very healthy and hardly ever seem to need a doctor. But of course we have some other parents in your profession, Nancy's father is a general practitioner at Worthing, and there is a little boy in the first form whose mother is a school medical officer, quite near your home, I think; in Hendon, or Golders Green. I will try to find a chance to introduce you later."

Since Harry could not even look grateful for the bright prospect she invoked for him Emma hurried into speech. "Our son has gone off with a charming girl, about seventeen, with a younger brother called Diggory."

"That will be Tess, she is very reliable. She has a most talented brother, you will hear him play in the concert this afternoon."

"We may not be able to stay so long," Harry said at once.

"Harry is off to Denmark tomorrow," Emma said, as if this might dispose of Harry's gruffness : and Janet saw that it almost did, for Emma. But she was not married to Harry and so was able to say in her light but definite voice.

"It will be a pity if you miss the concert. You will not have seen all that the children have to offer, and it is really a great deal. Perhaps we should go and find my brother, Emma. And I wonder if Professor Branksome would like to walk about a little and see the place for himself."

"Oh, that would be a good idea!" Emma cried. "Just look at everything, Harry, and I will talk to Janet about dull things like socks and baths and bedtimes."

Harry had the unfamiliar sense of being dismissed, a condition to which he had not been subjected for much longer than the whole of his son's life. Then he remembered that Janet had an older claim than his own on Emma, and his standing sense that his presence filled the whole of his wife's horizon suffered a tiny but important shock. He heard himself mutter something, he knew he turned away, and as he did so a young woman came out of the deep shadows along the back wall of the house, accompanied by a little girl in sweater and jeans. Both were of a disturbing beauty; the resemblance between them went so deep that it seemed only incidentally to take account of colouring or build. Another resemblance struck Harry at the same moment; this startling child in whom her mother seemed written too large for there to be room left for another signature was almost as much like the father she would not have known, whom Harry knew so well; his sister's husband, a philanderer.

VIII

"WHERE IS MY grandson?" Mrs. Daintry said, stepping out of her son-in-law's powerful car with an accusing glance which lacked an object in Daniel's absence. "Why isn't he here to welcome us? Does he think we have driven nearly two hundred miles to be ignored?"

"I expect he is sprucing himself up for you, mother," Vincent said pacifically. "He knows you like him to look presentable."

Mrs. Daintry's eye took in those of Daniel's friends who stood, sat or slouched around the courtyard in varying degrees of untidiness, or even of grandeur : she said nothing, there being no need.

"Shall we buy a magazine while we are waiting for him?" Dinah said. "Sit down here in the shade, Muriel dear, and I will bring you one."

The older woman sat down after examining the seat of the chair with a closeness of attention that drew a look of amusement from her son-in-law's wife, and one of annoyance from Florence who came towards her with a tray.

"Will you have a cup of tea or coffee?"

"No, thank you. I am just sitting here because there is nowhere else to sit. When you are my age you will be glad to sit down when you are waiting for somebody."

"You are Daniel's grandmother, aren't you?"

"Do you know where my grandson is? I think it very offhand of him not to be here to welcome us. However I daresay I expect too much. I daresay it is too much to expect of young people nowadays, a little common courtesy."

"Perhaps he will be here soon," Florence said, concealing a real doubt in an assumed one. "Daniel is always very polite," she offered.

"Always seems not appropriate, just when he is not being polite at all."

"Mother, look, here is a poem I should think Dan must have written," Vincent said, coming up with his copy of the magazine.

Mrs. Daintry read the poem.

"Is it good, Vincent? It seems quite good to me, for a boy of his age. Of course I know nothing about poetry, and Lawrence has never been one of my favourites. And how are we to know if Daniel wrote it? Is he ashamed of his work, not even putting his name to it?"

"Oh, Muriel, you know how shy these adolescents are!" Dinah said, with a kind look at Florence who turned away as if to bear out her words.

"No, I don't, Dinah. I know nothing whatever about adolescents. You and Vincent have convinced me that I am totally ignorant of the world my grandson is growing up in. And if a boy writes a poem and is not ashamed of it I should expect his name to be on it : I should think the editor might refuse contributions that cannot even be owned up to."

"Nearly all the poems are anonymous : if the editor had refused them the magazine would be half the size."

"How strange, when you tell me the place is so free and easy and offers so much opportunity for self expression! I would have thought anyone who had a little gift of expression would be encouraged to reveal himself in such an atmosphere. But I see that I was wrong : as usual I have taken too simple a view."

"Yes, Mother, you have."

Mrs. Daintry subsided with a snapping together of her lips that was almost audible, and Vincent and Dinah exchanged looks over her pretty hat.

"There is Miss Lindsay, Vincent. I wonder if she would know where Daniel has got to?"

Meg, who had walked the length of the courtyard under Harry's eyes and seen her child go off to wash and change, turned back as if to an ordeal that could not be avoided for much longer, but Vincent came up to her; she could not have explained the disappointment that attended this happy accident, any more than she could prevent herself looking quickly to see if Harry had moved during the minute or so that her back had been turned to him. He had not; he stood as if rooted between the cobbles, looking in her direction without disguise or apology. She smiled at him deprecatingly; she could not understand herself, smiling at Harry in any way at all, she could much better understand his immediately moving away towards a display of work in the geography room. In this divided state of mind she had also to think of a reply to Vincent's question, so casually asked but not casually to be answered.

"Daniel is not here this morning, Mr. Hardy."

"Not here?" Vincent said, raising his splendid eyebrows with a lively effect of surprise not long able to disturb his customary assurance. "Oh well, of course I know that; I mean, otherwise I would hardly have asked you."

"I mean he is not in the school. I think Janet would like to talk to you about him. Somebody is with her at the moment, but I will tell her you have arrived and then she will see you as soon as she is free."

"But, Miss Lindsay! That is all very well, but what am I to say to my wife, to the boy's grandmother? Not in the school, what does that mean?"

"He is somewhere nearby," Meg said, "and he is perfectly all right, there is no need for anybody to worry about him."

"No need to worry, I am very relieved to hear that; but I don't know that it will do for the ladies. Am I just to say to them that nobody knows where the boy is, but there is no need to worry?"

"I will say it for you, if you like."

"No, no, if anyone has to say anything it had better be me: give me a moment, talk to me for a minute or two, just while I think of some way of telling them whatever it is there is to tell. Has he run away, Miss Lindsay?"

"Really he has not. Please trust me, Mr. Hardy. I would not lie to you about anything so important, you know that Janet would never let me."

"If only we hadn't brought his grandmother with us," the man now groaned. "She likes to come, although she grumbles from beginning to end; and I don't know when we shall hear the last of this. It is really rather too bad of Dan, when he knows what she is like, better than anyone."

"I think you might safely tell Mrs. Daintry that he has gone off for a little while and will be back to see her later."

"Well, if you think it would be safe; but she will want to know why, and where, and for how long. I want to know those things myself."

"Tess!" Meg said, turning to the girl who now came up unhurriedly with Robert and a bag of crisps they were sharing, "would you go and tell Janet that Daniel's father is here?"

"I am supposed to be looking after this little boy," Tess said doubtfully.

"Take him with you. His mother is with Janet now."

"Shall we go to your mother?" Tess said to Robert, but Robert was looking at Vincent with fascination; the child's clutch on her fingers tightened.

"That is the man I was telling you about, there is his car. A big boy was hiding from him, I saw it from the hotel window."

"What big boy?" Vincent said in a peremptory voice.

Robert moved swiftly round to the far side of Tess, and Tess said in a tone of warning,

"Robert was telling me about something that happened last night. I think he must have seen Daniel in the village. Would you like some crisps, Meg?"

"No, Tess, thank you. Must you begin eating so early?"

"I have to practise at half past ten, and I don't know when Tim will let us go to lunch; so I thought I had better have something while I could. Would you like to finish them, Robert?"

Robert nodded, but would not open his mouth again in Vincent's presence. Tess gave him the bag and they went off together.

"Dan was in Newcastle Emlyn last night and saw us arrive, and hid from us?" Vincent said. "What is the matter with my son, Miss Lindsay?" Before she could answer, and indeed she could not answer, he turned and bellowed across the courtyard, "Dinah, come here a moment, Miss Lindsay wants to speak to you."

"I would not go if I were you, Dinah," Mrs. Daintry said. "It is not that young woman's place to issue orders right, left and centre. If I were you I would just smile politely and let her come here if she has anything to say."

"It is Vincent who wants me, I rather think," Dinah said. "I will be back in a moment, Muriel." And to her husband a moment later, "What is it? Has something happened to Dan?"

Vincent looked at Meg, who said nothing.

"Nothing alarming has happened. Janet will be coming to talk to us. It sounds as if Dan doesn't want to see us, if you can conceive of such a thing."

There were few things Dinah could not conceive of, and Daniel's defection was not among them.

"Oh, Vincent, really, there is no need to look so stunned! You know very well how unpredictable boys of Daniel's age can be. There was Terry—remember what a time the school had with him, six or seven episodes ago."

"But this is a real boy, my son, and a real school. This is actually happening, Dinah, Daniel is hiding from us!"

"Yes, it is thrilling to see how right we were about Terry; remember how horrified his parents were—they felt they had done everything for him and then the boy simply cut himself off; we were absolutely on the ball there, Vincent; their reaction was exactly what yours is now, ours, I ought to say."

"What was their reaction?" Janet said, coming up with a look of warm interest and a nod to Meg, which Meg took as her order of release.

"Oh, Miss Storace! Now everything will be all right. Here is my husband you see, quite baffled and trembling, the very first time he actually has to deal with an adolescent crisis, the kind of thing we write about almost every week."

"Writing is not quite the same," Janet said, "and a school where this happened every week would be in a bad way."

"Ah, but Cilrheddyn is such a small school. If you had fourteen hundred children you would expect twelve times as many difficulties."

"I don't think I would. There would be so many more people to deal with them."

Dinah laughed; that pleasing sound reached Emma's ears as she rejoined her husband.

"Where is Robert?" Harry said at once. "Is he still with that girl? I saw her give him a bag of crisps; he will eat no lunch today."

"He has gone off with Janet's brother, with Matthew, I mean, I find it awkward to call him that when I have only seen him just the once."

"Call him Mr. Storace then, as you would any other head-master. That is what he is, after all, a headmaster."

"Yes," Emma said, and was silent. During her silence, Harry's thought really alighted upon what she had just told him, the haze of his disapproval cleared for just long enough for him to see clearly an impossible picture; his child going off, whatever that might mean, with a strange man.

"Gone off? Gone off where, with this Matthew, then? He will be crying, you know he does not like to be away from you."

"He was happy enough with the girl, when they went to see the rabbits. He wanted to show the rabbits to Mr. Storace."

"Who must have been very eager to see them in Robert's company! Did Robert suppose that he would never have seen them before?"

"Yes, and he was right, Harry, because there were young ones; and Tess said, the girl said, today is the first time they have come out into the run."

Harry digested all this, and found there was little in it to justify his lack of ease.

"What are we supposed to do now, then? Has Miss Storace finished with you?"

"She had to speak to Mr. and Mrs. Hardy: and she wanted us to look round—everywhere she said, dormitories, lavatories, classrooms, all over the place."

"It sounds as if she were trying to prove there is nothing she need be ashamed of," Harry said, not without some shame of his own.

"There is an exhibition in the library, French poetry in the nineteenth century, and the children have made a study of local wild life, their notebooks and drawings are in the biology room, up those stairs. Shall we go and see that first?"

Before they could go anywhere Dinah came up to them.

"Have you seen everything? Should we show you round? Vincent just has to explain something to Muriel, she is in rather a state. I don't know if you have heard," she said, addressing herself to Harry, as if the thing might best be kept from Emma's notice, "my step-son has taken it into his head to run away."

"To run away, Mrs. Hardy?" Emma said, with a frightened look at Harry.

"Oh, he used to do it all the time," Dinah said with no

alteration in her manner. "The first year at his other school he popped up and down like a jack in the box. Then he came here and gave it up. Or we thought he had."

"Is he a tall boy," Harry now said, "with yellow hair and dark brows and eyes, very thin?"

"Yes, that would be Daniel, he is not at all like Vincent, Muriel says he is just like her daughter as a girl. It is so much safer at a co-educational school for boys with Daniel's looks. But how did you know?" Dinah said, in a suddenly suspicious tone, as if she felt that Harry had kept something from her, a thing she preferred nobody even to try to do.

"We saw a boy like that in Newcastle Emlyn last night," Harry said. "He was eating fish and chips out of a newspaper."

"The plot thickens!" Dinah cried. "He knew what time we would be arriving, he knew where we would spend the night. It is almost as if he had to make sure that we were there. Only why didn't he come to us?" Harry and Emma could offer no explanation, but Dinah made up for this at once and in generous measure. "We must have made some ghastly mistake somewhere; parents usually do, and ours is not an ordinary family. I wonder if he feels I have displaced him in his father's affections? If he were a girl that is the very first thing one would think of. Or of course there is the simple resentment he must have felt at my taking his mother's place. And I am nearer his age than his father's, which creates another difficulty, especially now he is growing up so fast. And his grandmother is no help, she is really an awful nuisance in some ways; she never stops to think what she is saying, and some of her thoughts would be much better kept to herself."

She finished; the rapidity of her own thoughts had left her breathless.

"I am very sorry," Emma said inadequately.

"Why should you be?" Dinah said, the tears springing to her eyes. "It is not your fault. Only it does make me feel such a fool when I can't understand my own step-son and we have always got on so well."

She dabbed fiercely at her eyes with her handkerchief, thrust it back into her handbag, and crossed the courtyard to Muriel with a perceptible squaring of her slight shoulders.

"How sad, Harry! What an awful situation for the poor girl!"

"Oh, for God's sake, Emma, you cannot start carrying her burdens as well as your own. Surely you have problems enough with Robert; leave Mrs. Hardy to worry about her step-son. She has theories enough to explain his behaviour; she ought to be able to think up a way of dealing with it."

"I don't think," Emma said slowly, "that I feel sorry for her because of the boy. Anyone can see that she likes him very much. But the old lady; I would not like to have to account for everything to an old lady like that."

"She looks nice enough," Harry said with a swift look at Mrs. Daintry.

"Do you think so? I saw her at the breakfast table, watching Robert, and every time his voice rose or he dropped his napkin she seemed to notice it."

"You were imagining things, Emma. You know how embarrassed you get when the boy plays up in public. And even if she did notice him and disapprove that hardly makes her into a monster. I find him irritating enough and I am his father."

"But women generally make allowances for children away from home," Emma said. "She spoke to him as we went out of the dining room and he looked frightened; afterwards he told me some strange tale about her taking him into her room and giving him a biscuit before breakfast: before we were awake, he said."

"Perhaps it was true. And that sounds as if she were kinder than you like to think her. If I were Mrs. Hardy I should probably say that you were jealous because another woman had done a kindness to your son and felt it gave her a claim upon him."

Emma started as if she had been stung, but Harry had noticed one of Peter's posters.

"We have been here nearly an hour and seen nothing: shall we look at the local wild life you spoke of? Or would you rather go to the library first?"

"There is coffee in the library," Emma pointed out, so that was where they went.

"So we have come all the way down here for nothing." Muriel said. "That is what you are trying to tell me, I suppose. And I will not pretend I am surprised. I have seen the writing on the wall, though you have not. Another kind of writing has taken up too much of your time. I knew the boy was not happy; I have known it for many months."

"It is a great pity that you kept the knowledge to yourself, then," Vincent said, allowing his exasperation room to breathe, which it must have if he were not to burst; the sun's heat striking up from the smooth rounded cobbles, bouncing back off the stone walls and flashing windows, the airless well of the court-yard thickening now with noise as other cars drove in and other children, other parents, added their greetings, cries, laughter, news, caresses to all that was there already, including his dead wife's mother in her terrible satisfied anger and his new young wife in such pain : it was too much, he could not stand it without his boy, the sole reason for his appearance in such a place, at such a time. He put up his head and bellowed at his womenfolk, not unaware that heads all round came up too at the sound of his voice; up from the perusal of magazines, the selection of pots, the inspection of dresses put on with pride for the first time or socks seen to be in need of darning by mothers happily knowing themselves not yet superseded. "If you knew Dan was having a bad time of it," Vincent now shouted, "why in God's name did you have to keep it to yourself?"

Florence came out with her tray and a look of resourceful-ness.

"Will you have a cup of tea or coffee, Mr. Hardy, while you are waiting? Mrs. Hardy, would you like a biscuit? The plain ones are three for a penny; they are quite nice, the third formers made them yesterday afternoon."

Vincent snatched a cup from the tray and gave it to his wife who took it in unaccustomed silence.

"I will have a cup, too, please," Muriel said in a demure tone. And more demurely still, "There is no need for you to raise your voice to me, Vincent. My hearing has got no worse with age. You know now my judgement has not."

Florence set a cup of tea in front of her.

"That will be a shilling, if you don't want any biscuits."

Vincent fought with the change in his pockets and captured the right coin : Florence took it, and added with her eyes on the ground, "Daniel is not especially unhappy. He had a row with Jude Pinnegar, that is all. And he did not write the Lawrence poem, I did. He wrote some of the others; I think so, at least, because I didn't."

She whisked back into the shadowed safety of the art room.

"Who is Jude Pinnegar?" Muriel said, sipping her tea with an air of restraint.

"Tess's brother," Dinah said. "The boy who plays in all the concerts. You will remember him from last year."

"I remember the lovely music, dear I don't recall the faces, I prefer to listen with my eyes closed. But naturally I know of the Pinnegars, there are so many of them. He must be a very disagreeable boy, to upset Daniel so."

"Oh, Muriel, you must not take what that girl said too literally. She knows nothing about it."

"She knows nothing, I know nothing," Muriel said, and rocked herself delicately back and forth on her hard chair. "Only you and Vincent know, I suppose: and your knowledge seems to be doing you very little good."

"There is Tess," Dinah said eagerly, as the girl came out of the art room with a plate of biscuits and a glass full of red fluid with a straw in it. "Can you spare us a moment, Tess?"

"Good morning, Mrs. Hardy. I can, if it is only a moment, and if you don't mind my going on eating while you talk to me. I have to rehearse in about five minutes, and I am starving. I was too excited to eat much breakfast: I bought a bag of crisps but a little boy ate most of them."

She sat down with a look of simple envy for Dinah's linen suit and a quick glance at her own cotton frock which seemed suddenly too short, too tight, too limp, too red.

"Go ahead. How lucky you are to be seventeen and able to gorge if you feel like it!"

Tess frowned, but Dinah missed the frown, as she missed everything not in her immediate path, and went on with her look of expectancy, "They tell us your brother and Daniel have had a quarrel and that is why Dan isn't here just now."

"They had a quarrel," Tess said, between two long pulls at her straw.

"Was it anything we should know about?"

"I expect Dan will tell you when you see him."

"When will we see him?" Muriel said, tapping a gloved finger sharply on the table before her "Can you tell us that, young lady? That is all we want to know, though nobody has the ordinary honesty to say so."

"I don't know," Tess said, pushing her glass away with a gesture of revulsion which seemed to extend beyond the crimson syrup it had contained.

"Because we have come all the way from London, at great expense, and stayed overnight at an hotel, which is by no means cheap, in order to see my grandson : these are things that he seems not to have considered, treating us in this shabby way. I am sure you would not treat your relations like that, would you?"

"I don't know," Tess said again in desperation, conscious of three pairs of eyes upon her; Dinah's dark and bright, Vincent's pale and bewildered, the old lady's of no definite colour, but watchful. Her thoughts flew to real recriminations, to anger, to Jude. "I have to go, they will be waiting for me in the music room."

"Will your brother be there?" Vincent said, almost in a tone of apology. "Might I speak to him, do you think?"

"He doesn't like to talk before he plays," Tess said; panic over-came her. "Tim won't let him be disturbed," she added, and with this notion that had no substance in any attitude of Tim's, safety seemed restored; she felt the warm sun again and saw her friends; there was Nancy selling a beaker, Florence mopping up spilt coffee, handsome Peter taking his parents off to the science block, Janet admiring somebody's baby sister. "Perhaps later on," she said with confidence, "after the concert, I daresay you could talk to him."

"I am sure we shall be grateful for the privilege," Mrs. Daintry said.

"Mother, there is no need to be like that," Vincent said. "Whatever has happened Tess is not to blame."

"I never said she was, dear. Dinah, did I suggest anything of the kind?"

"I think your manner did suggest it, just a little, Muriel."

"Then I apologise," Muriel said with an air of doing the right thing in the face of difficulties. "You will understand that I am worried and disappointed. I thought that I spoke for all of us, but it seems that I was mistaken."

Vincent made a strangled sound and Dinah said very quickly, "There are your people now, Tess. Off you go!"

Tess needed no urging, running to Tamsin, to Helen, above all to her father whose drawn face escaped her notice, though he could read the strain in hers.

"Why, Tess, dear, whatever is wrong?"

"Nothing. Oh, I am so glad you are here! Tim is waiting for us in the music room. Diggory is around somewhere, Mum. Tamsin, how tall you are. Can you have grown since sports day?"

"No, this is last year's dress," Tamsin said. "I told you it was too short," she said to Helen in a fierce whisper. "I told you everyone would notice."

"Hush, Tamsin, there is nothing to be done about it now."

"You should have let me wear my shorts. I did to Sports Day."

"Parents' Day is different. People put on special clothes for a special day."

"Last year's dress is not special."

"Gracious!" Tess cried. "I thought you would be pleased if I said you had grown. Usually you like it."

"If you only say it because you think I like it, there is no point in your ever saying it again."

"She is tired, Tess," Helen said parenthetically. "We got up so early, and she didn't sleep in the car."

"There is a little boy somewhere," Tess said, "who might be coming here next year or the year after: you would like to play with him."

"No, thank you," Tamsin said. "I shall wait for Diggory."

"Where is Jude?" her mother asked, a long look around the courtyard having shown her no glimpse of her older son.

"He is with Tim. Come to the library and have some coffee and then Daddy and I will have to practise."

Tess put her arm through her father's and kissed his cheek: this felt different from Daniel's.

"How bristly you are!"

"I shaved before six. Perhaps Jude will lend me a razor before the concert."

"He will have to, or somebody might mistake you for Mr. Hardy."

Owen's glance rested on Vincent, a dozen yards away.

"I don't think there is any risk. He is twice my size."

"Do people shrink as they get older?" Tess said. "You look smaller to me now than I remember your being."

"You are getting bigger yourself all the time," her mother said.

Tess held her father at arm's length and examined him with love, which was not as blind as it is generally supposed.

"No, I am wrong. You are not smaller exactly, only thinner. Your cheeks are thinner. Are you slimming?"

"Not intentionally," Owen said with a wary look at Helen.

"We are," Tess said, "at least we are all trying to; I am lucky, I can eat anything, but Kate has to cut out potatoes and toast at breakfast, and I eat less toast to keep her company. Then I eat her potato at lunchtime to make up for it. Janet doesn't like it, she says young people need their strength, but Kate is strong enough for anything she wants to do."

Owen saw that his daughter's attention had left him for the moment and was able to relax.

"I will just get my violin out of the boot, and then we must go and say a word to Janet before I come to the music room."

"I will get it, Daddy. Honestly, you look terrible. If you are worrying about the concert you need not. Tim is going to explain beforehand so nobody will expect a very high standard."

"Bring the violin, Tess," Helen said, quite sharply, for her "Tamsin, we are going to the library now. I will see you later, when you find Diggory. You may give him his jumper. Come along now, Owen."

She took her husband's hand and they walked at a sedate pace across the courtyard, up a shallow flight of steps and through an open door beneath one of Peter's signs. Tess followed with the fiddle and a crestfallen look : for she had suddenly guessed that her parents, though they were scarcely a yard away, had left her far behind, and were exploring together some territory to which she possessed no map, no guidebook, and where the signposts were written in a foreign tongue.

IX

"OUR NEW FRIEND Mr. Hardy might look like that fellow in twenty years' time," Harry said, examining a photograph of Paul Verlaine with an attempt at interest. "Is it a writer's sort of face, Emma? This one was a writer, I take it; I don't know the name, but I suppose that poem is his."

The poem was a melancholy one, copied out in a beautiful italic hand, with a translation appended. " 'Rain falls in my heart,' " Harry now read. "Why were they all so gloomy, those chaps?"

Emma was pleased to be asked as though she would naturally be an authority on poets and their natures; her pleasure was not due to satisfied vanity, or to a wish to instruct her husband in a field where his ignorance exceeded by howsoever little her own, but to a just appreciation of his concession to the day, the place, and the preparations made for them. She had not dared to count on any such concessions, any more than she would have dared to hope that they would find themselves free of their child, drinking rather good coffee, and inspecting serenely enough the results of Celia's work with the older pupils.

"Daniel Hardy did our translations," Celia said, coming over to them as some other parents left her. "Don't you think they are good?"

"My French is too shaky for me to tell," Emma said sadly. "Certainly they read very well, almost as if they were originals."

"They are very free translations, of course."

"Of course," Harry said, with an ironic glance at his wife.

"But for the symbolists that always seems to me better than trying to be too literal. With Rimbaud's prose poems, the position is different."

"Is that Rimbaud?" Harry said with a jerk of his head at another picture : a wreath of columbines enclosed a face as delicate and charming as a girl's with light curls flowing to the throat.

"Isn't he absolutely fabulous?" Kate said. "Celia, Ian's mother asked if she could have a word with you. Poor Celia," she remarked to Harry, "everybody is out for her blood. The O-level papers were awful, we shall all have failed: the parents think it is because we spent so much time on this sort of thing, background studies, Celia calls it, instead of conjugating *avoir* from morning to night."

"This sort of thing must be much more interesting," Emma said.

"It is of real educational value," Kate said with a primness she sometimes borrowed from Florence.

"But learning the grammar of a language might be of value, too," Harry said, mildly enough.

"It would be best to learn both," Kate said, returning to her usual manner, "and some of us do. Celia tries her hardest. She has only been here a year, so she really is not to blame if our irregular verbs are shaky. After nearly half a century," she said to Harry with a rapid effort of assessment Nancy would have thought quite beyond her, "do you remember your pluperfects?"

"After less than half a century I cannot honestly say that I do."

"But in fifty years' time," Kate said in pretty triumph, "I shall probably remember Verlaine jumping on his wife when she was pregnant because she didn't like him to make love to Rimbaud, and Rimbaud tearing up lovely books in his friends' houses to use for bog-paper."

"Kate, love," Peter said, "your people are here; I saw them coming up the drive. You should not take too much notice of what Kate says," he told Emma kindly, "she was thought to be practically ineducable at one time, but you can see how wrong that was; it is just that she only learns what appeals to her."

"I would have thought that was true of most people," Harry said, "and it seems to leave out of account such trifling matters as public examinations and professional training."

"I can't see Kate wanting professional training," Peter said, "and even if she is to spend all her days pushing a pram or washing the dishes Cilrheddyn will have enlarged her horizons."

"To the extent of knowing a prurient tale or two about a couple of tenth rate foreign poets," Harry said to Emma in a quiet tone of disdain.

"But what they wrote was so beautiful, Harry."

"If your French is as poor as you told that young woman in green, how do you know that what they wrote is beautiful?"

"Creative people have often lived irregular lives."

"So have other people, only fewer excuses are made for them."

Emma looked desperately about, knowing that the blessed softening of mood that seemed to have come upon Harry so short a time before had failed to withstand the impact of several alien ideas and the candour of two young people who had spoken to him as if he might be one of themselves. The shabby library had seemed quiet and cool at their entrance, and quiet after the turmoil in the courtyard, but it was filling rapidly now with teachers and parents, with children on errands, real or imagined, with Spaniards carrying trays of clean cups, and with Meg who was supervising the Spaniards.

"Oh, Harry, there is Miss Lindsay, how very much she is changed!"

"I saw her before, when you were with Miss Storace."

"Did you? You never said so," Emma cried in a tone her husband took to contain an accusation, though Emma actually felt no more than the gentlest surprise at his reserve, dismissed the moment it was aired; since, after all, their morning had been full, and there had been little time for confidences. She could not have accounted for the further darkening of Harry's mood; he did not understand it himself, being only aware that something in his wife's earlier words had flicked him as if with the lightest of lashes.

"I did not think her so much changed. She is nearly ten years older, we all are."

"She has cut her hair. How strange, when I have grown mine again. I am almost sure mine was short the last time I saw her."

"She may have grown it and cut it again half a dozen times in ten years: there is nothing to be made of that. She has lived her own life, apart from us."

"Of course," Emma said, "and it cannot have been very easy for her."

"You did your best to make it easier. She owes you something, Emma, I hope she realises it."

His vehemence, uttering these words, seemed disproportionate: she turned back to the table where the fruits of Celia's misguided efforts were displayed. This time her gaze fell on a reproduced portrait of Baudelaire and a jacket design for *Les Fleurs du Mal,* loosely derived from Beardsley. As possible topics these seemed as dangerous as any, but what topic was safe with Harry now?

"Ian did the jacket," Peter said kindly. "It is a print, and copies are on sale for three shillings each. He wrote out the poems too, and the translations."

"He has been kept busy," Emma said with a little laugh that sounded to her own ears fatuous, but could not have been stifled : she had to laugh if she were not to shiver, her husband beside her now being cold as ice.

"Yes, he is in the Lower Sixth, so he has had no exams this year. It is the same with Tess, she is playing in the concert this afternoon and half the demonstrations in the physics lab. are hers."

"It might be kind," Harry said to Emma, cutting across the boy's last words in a peremptory manner, "if you were to have a word with Miss Lindsay when the chance offers."

"She is busy just now," Emma said. "She looks as if she has no time to spare."

"I daresay there will be a moment during the afternoon. They cannot expect her to spend all her time chasing children and domestics, a girl of her gifts. And I would not like her to think we were avoiding her."

"You don't think she might prefer to be avoided?" Emma suggested, and regretted the words almost before they were uttered.

"No, I do not; being in this place must be a sort of exile for her. She will be glad to see a familiar face, two familiar faces, if she remembers me at all."

Emma suppressed a second urge to laugh since there was no excuse available now for laughter : Peter had moved away to talk to Celia, she could not use the boy to cover her acute sense of what was ridiculous in Harry's words. To suppose, as he evidently did, that after nine or more years, a third nearly of the young woman's lifetime, Meg should look for comfort to two people hardly known to her before, save as the woman who had urged her to destroy her baby and the brother of that other woman whose husband she had seduced! "Envoys from the beloved homeland," Emma now said, looking Harry full in the face. "Do you imagine that is how Meg Lindsay will see us?"

"It is only right to give her the chance to do so," Harry said, and justice seemed to be on his side, if discretion and sensibility were on her own.

"Well, I will try, Harry. But I am not going to drive her into a corner and make it impossible for her to get away. If the opportunity comes naturally and easily I will take it."

"That is all I ever asked for," he said. "When the chance offers, was how I put it. You are making an absurd fuss over nothing at all."

"I hope you are not worrying over your little boy, Mrs. Branksome," Muriel said, coming up to them in time to catch Harry's last words; she was adept at retrieving such trifles, having long since learned how much busier people than herself would throw away.

"Have you seen him?" Emma asked eagerly, greeting a familiar worry as an old friend, much to be preferred to the newer doubts aroused by Harry's strangeness.

"No, but he can come to no harm here. Nothing is forbidden, there are no rules to break, nothing could be shabbier or more decrepit than it is already."

"Robert is with Mr. Storace: I should not think he will damage anything."

"When I think," the older woman said, brushing aside Emma's words, "when I remember, for my memory has not failed me yet, what houses like this were in my girlhood! The care that was lavished on them! How fortunate that those of us who recall such things will soon be passed away; only a few more years and nobody will suffer as I suffer now, seeing neglect and callous disregard for beauty everywhere."

"But nobody chooses to neglect these places," Emma cried. "Surely it is just the expense, the lack of labour?"

"There is money enough for some things," Mrs. Daintry said significantly. "There is enough and to spare for trips to the moon and false teeth for everyone and foreigners using our hospitals. And enough for some of the children here to have their fees paid out of the rates; my son-in-law pays rates and taxes and school fees too; all over the country great boys and girls who ought to be at work are staying on at school at his expense and yours, for that matter, or at least your husband's. Professor Branksome, do you feel it right and reasonable that some people should pay not a penny towards the fees of a school like this?"

But Harry had not been listening. Muriel repeated her question with additions.

"Why should it be free for some, while others pay so much? There is one family, I will not name them, of course—I happen to know that the oldest girl is here because she had asthma as a child; it was all over before she came to Cilrheddyn, but her fees are paid. Then they sent her brother after her; no doubt it was easy to find some reason that would satisfy the local authority. The boy is said to be a fine young musician, he is certainly very disagreeable, so perhaps they found a doctor to say he was maladjusted. You would think they would be ashamed, decent people would, I am sure : and now there is another boy here, and a second girl to come. The father is only a teacher, and we all know what teachers are paid."

"Perhaps they have made great sacrifices for their children," Emma said, as Harry seemed not to want to say anything at all.

"Sacrifice! What does anybody know of sacrifice today? When I was a girl if a young man wanted an education and his parents had no money he worked all day at his trade and all night at his books. He was not to be taught at the public expense. Nobody values what is not paid for; I have not lived more than seventy years without learning that."

"Here you are Muriel," Dinah said, with mock severity overlying a real severity. "We have been looking for you everywhere, as if it is not enough that Daniel is missing."

"I wanted a little shade," Muriel said in a tone of weakness quite different from the pettish but lively one she had been using a moment before. "The children were noisy and I do not like cobbles or hard chairs."

"Vincent thinks we should go back to the hotel for lunch as if everything were just as usual. Daniel might turn up at any time."

"Has he spoken to that boy, that Jude Pinnegar?"

"No, Janet said he should not. And she said she saw Daniel this morning in the church down the hill : she thinks he should be left alone to come back when he is ready."

"We are to miss our boy half the day or more, because she thinks so, is that it?"

"She does understand young people awfully well, Muriel."

"Well, I should hope so, when she is in charge of so many

of them. What does her brother make of all this, I should like to know?"

"I have not seen Matthew, he is out in the grounds somewhere, but Janet says he believes that Daniel has been brooding on something all this term, and this silly scene with Jude yesterday was only the last straw."

"Oh, they all take that young man's part," Muriel said with quiet scorn. "His feelings are sacred, you observe: he is not to be spoken to in case he is upset, but our boy can worry himself sick for weeks on end and we are simply to leave him alone. I am not so sure we should do as we are told; we are not pupils here after all, and even the pupils only obey Janet when they feel like it. I heard her telling some of the children that only parents were allowed in the library, and now the place is swarming with them."

"Oh, Muriel! Naturally they want to be with their mothers when they can. Janet was only trying to keep the numbers within bounds."

"There is the Lindsay child," Muriel said, "and that girl Tess and her parents and their younger children, the ones I mentioned to you, Professor Branksome. You would think anyone would know better than to crowd the place out with unwanted children."

"What children? What unwanted children?" Harry said in a suddenly rough voice. His attention had left Muriel long before, and her words, disconnected altogether from their context struck his ear with a meaning they did not really possess. She had sat down and now stared up at him with frightened eyes; his wife put a hand on his arm and murmured something placatory. Dinah Hardy said above Emma's murmur in a matter-of-fact way,

"What are the lovely things on this table? Oh, look, Muriel, how clever. These are Dan's translations, that he was telling Vincent about in the Easter holidays: Vincent promised him he would get someone at the B.B.C. to have a look at them. I don't know if anything came of it."

"Nothing would come of it," Mrs. Daintry said, her tone now sombre. "Vincent is always so busy; let me see what our boy has written."

She stood up, resting her hands on the table, and began to

intone Rimbaud's words, and her grandson's, and some lines of Verlaine's. She had a pretty accent; in the pleasure of listening to herself she forgot the shock Harry had given her with his inexplicable sharpness. In that part of her mind which acted as a capacious receptacle for all that displeased her she had nevertheless tucked away the bad manners of this new acquaintance, along with Jude Pinnegar's arrogance, his indigent family, and Janet's tacit claim to know more about Daniel than his own grandmother.

"How beautifully she reads!" Tess said to her mother in an audible whisper. "Those are Daniel's translations, Mum. Don't you think they are good?"

"Get your father a cup of coffee, darling, will you?" Helen said. "And Diggory, Tamsin, run along now: I am sure you should not be in here. I will come out to you as soon as Daddy goes to the music room."

"Do you want your biscuit?" Diggory asked Owen, as Tess came back with a cup and a plate, which Owen took without looking at what was on it.

"No, you may have it, and then do as your mother says. I shall only be a few minutes, Tess, if you will just tell Tim I shall be coming."

"Of course I will," Tess said and left them, taking Tamsin by the hand: Diggory followed, concealing his biscuit, but not from Muriel, who weighed what she had heard Tess say against what she had seen Diggory do, and was pleased to find that her own gratification was of no account and she could still find the Pinnegars intolerable.

"Vincent, dear," she suggested to her son-in-law a little later when he had finished talking to Janet, to Celia, to Meg, to several other teachers, for he believed in being generous with his splendid voice and presence, and would not lower his public standards for any private woe, "would it be a good idea to ask Professor Branksome and his wife to join us at luncheon? I do not mean a formal invitation, of course, I would not like to involve you in any expense: but just a suggestion that our tables at the hotel might be moved together?"

"Certainly, mother, if you would like it."

"It is not what I would like, dear, it is doing the right thing, showing a friendly interest in these people who must be feeling a little strange in a place like this. Mrs. Branksome says nothing, but I can see that she is ill at ease; and her husband frowns and frowns; I think he very likely shares my views on Cilrheddyn."

"I will gladly ask them to lunch with us, mother, but not if you intend to start complaining about the school. That would upset Dinah, in the circumstances."

"Poor child!" Muriel said with full complacency. "She has always thought so well of the place : this morning has been a blow for her. And for you, too, dear, though you say so little. I know what you are going through, and I think some cheerful conversation at the luncheon table would help us all."

"Where have they got to, then?" Vincent said, bowing to her inexorable will with a good grace.

"They were here just a moment ago. I dare say they fled when the Pinnegars arrived."

"I can see Mrs. Branksome, she is with Meg Lindsay. Dinah will look after you while I ask her."

There seemed nothing that Emma could say to Meg Lindsay that would not set them both blushing; but the eddying movement of parents and children around the tables had finally brought them face to face. Here was the chance offered that Harry had told her she must seize; here equally was the occasion for an apparent avoidance that both women would greatly have preferred but knew must not be taken.

"It is very crowded in here," Emma said. "Preparing for so many people must take a lot of your time, Miss Lindsay."

"It is what I am paid for, among other things. And it is only once a year. We all enjoy it, though we grumble."

"I think I saw your little girl," Emma now said, and feared that Meg might think the child's likeness to her father had aided recognition. "She is so like you, her hair is nearly the same colour as yours."

Meg knew what Emma had feared, and liked and despised her both at once for trying to conceal her fear, and doing it so clumsily.

"She must be nearly the same age as Robert," Emma said.

"Yes, I was two months' pregnant when you met me outside Mr. Murivance's."

"I suppose you must have been," Emma said, as though she might really have supposed something different.

"Where is your son now?" Meg said, with the intention of covering her own embarrassment as well as relieving Emma's.

"Mr. Storace has taken him for a walk in the grounds. They have been together nearly half an hour. I hope Robert is behaving himself."

"Going for a walk with Matthew is just going for a walk," Meg said. "He will not be put to any test. If any questions are asked, your son will be asking them."

"Harry—my husband finds it all so strange, the Christian names, the informality."

"Everyone does at first, but of course it comes naturally to most of the children. In an ordinary prep. school your little boy would be called Branksome; that is much more unnatural for a child."

"He has been called that," Emma said, and felt a sudden deep shame that she could ever have thought such a practice sound, or even tolerable.

"Meg, dear, may I interrupt you, just for one moment?" Vincent said, putting an arm round Meg's shoulders; this was easy enough to do as her head barely reached his own shoulders, and seemed so natural a gesture that Emma's immediate revulsion took some accounting for, when she later considered it. "She arouses this urge in men to touch and hold her; and she does it absolutely without coquetry. It is a strange power to exert almost against one's will, and it must be that when she knows so well what it can lead to. But why should I attach any importance to it? It was not Harry, it was a man who is virtually a stranger to me who touched her so carelessly, and yet I felt that touch as a blow to myself."

But at the time her recoil was invisible, no change in her expression revealed it to Vincent, or to Meg, who smiled and moved away with words that fitted the situation and added nothing to it.

"My mother-in-law wanted me to suggest a plan for our luncheon. We shall be without our son, and my wife, of course, feels it : and in short we should be very grateful if you and your husband could join us at the hotel, if you were thinking of going back there."

Emma's thoughts went to Robert, and to Muriel's glances at breakfast.

"It is very kind of you, Mr. Hardy. Harry seems to have disappeared, I expect he has gone to find our son. Will you allow me to go after him, and give you an answer later?"

"Why, of course, Mrs. Branksome : there is no need for an answer at all. We shall simply be in the hotel dining room at one, and if you are there, well and good. If you are not, we shall take it that you have other plans. Now, where did Meg go? I just wondered if she might take me up to Daniel's dormitory, in case there is anything to be discovered there."

Vincent in fact found Meg with greater facility than Emma found her husband. She left the library, traversed a labyrinth of corridors, looking into changing rooms and laboratories, rooms where trays of food covered with white muslin were waiting to be taken to the courtyard for afternoon tea or the sale of work; she crossed the courtyard, made sure that Harry was not in their car, passed the pottery stall, almost bare, and the art room, full of people, their voices a steady hum, punctuated now and then by sharper sounds, pride of parents, deprecating shrieks of daughters who thought their gratification should not be suspected. Emma's eyes at last fell on a notice she had not seen before; it bore the symbol of a pacifist organisation in black and white, and an arrow in red, pointing away from the courtyard towards a row of outbuildings; some of stone, as old as the house; some of wood, raw and ugly. Over the doorway of one of these sheds, for really it was no more than that, the symbol was repeated. "Harry would not have gone in there," Emma said, but went in to make sure.

Her husband was there; the benches of this cramped workshop had been cleared and there were piles of pamphlets lying upon them. On the walls photographs had been pinned, not very straight : a baby with a stomach as large as his head and limbs together, a woman with shrunken breasts holding another baby, mercifully dead. Bodies without skin, faces without eyes, limbs without digits, monstrosities that only shreds of clothing identified as human, adorned a notice board, together with the slogans of the movement, pictures of jet aircraft, of mushroom clouds, of soldiers interrogating prisoners, of powerful men whose sleep these matters must be supposed not greatly to disturb. Emma came close to Harry, and a thrill of terror ran through her; it was not that she had never seen these things before, she was no more able to close her eyes and mind to them than any other woman : it was the black ugliness of the contrast they pointed in this sunny place, where the young were to be fed in body and spirit, and made fit for life in a world so little fit for them.

There were some bars of music, copied large on a sheet of cartridge paper, the notes as big as apples, the words that fitted them lettered in a different hand from the beautiful one that had copied out Daniel Hardy's translations; the black paint had dripped, run and smeared. Neither Emma nor her husband recognised the music, which was Britten's, or the words, which were Eric Crozier's, and represented the plaint of another child in another world, not after all less terrible.

" 'How should I laugh and play?' " Emma read aloud. She did not look at Harry, but felt his arm about her. A voice from the sunlit doorway said,

"Here is your mother, Robert. Mrs. Branksome, here is your son."

Emma stepped forward at once, lest Robert should see what she had just seen; but the child was standing a yard or two away, holding something with great care.

"Look, Mum, a girl has lent me a mouse! It is hers, one of hers, she has ever so many; and I may look after it until we go home. Matthew says I can have lunch here at the school, while you go back to the hotel, and the mouse can come too, in a box with holes in for breathing. Is that all right?"

He ended on a note of doubt, as Harry followed Emma out of the shed, but Harry smiled and allowed his smile to include Matthew standing there with another child dancing up and down by his side.

"It is my mouse," Meg's daughter said. "Can we go and find a box now, Matthew? Shall I take Robert to find one with me?"

"Yes, if his mother says you may."

"And may I have lunch here?" Robert begged.

"You had better," Harry said, "if you want to have a mouse on the table."

"Mummy?"

"Yes, dear, of course," Emma said.

X

"THAT WAS BETTER : that was probably as good as we can make it. I think we had better go on to the minuet, and if we have any time left over we can go back to your rising scale passages between bars thirty and forty, Mr. Pinnegar : they could be just a little smoother even than you made them. But actually we are not used to hearing them played so well."

Owen was glad to hear Tim's words for the sake of his son and daughter. He did not suppose them to be true : in his own performance he could hear only the glaring faults, right notes poorly sounded, ornamentation attempted with diffidence and achieved sketchily if at all.

"Jude, your appoggiatura in bar twenty-one was feeble : it was touch and go if you would get to the G on the first beat of the next bar."

"Sorry."

"Let us try the minuet then. We will play all the repeats, Mr. Pinnegar."

They tried the minuet, playing all the repeats. Afterwards there was silence, and nobody looked at anyone else.

"Perhaps we should try leaving out the grace notes in the first trio," Tim said.

"I think I can manage the grace notes," Owen said. "It is the syncopation in the inner voices that puts me off, and the run of descending sixths in the forty-fourth bar."

"Shall we do the first trio again? We had better leave the rest, or we shall have no time for the variations."

Jude sat back, resting his clarinet on his knees. The second trio was a show piece for his instrument, he had no part at all in the first. Owen's fiddle and Ian's sang to each other, swooping up and down, while the viola and 'cello crooned gently below them ; then Ian played quiet thirds while Owen managed, precariously, his failing sixths. They did better than on the first occasion, better still at the repeat.

"It won't be so bad," Tim said. "Really it is not bad at all."

"If we only had a little longer to practise!" Tess sighed.

"After Matthew's speech?" Ian suggested; he was a thin, flattened-looking boy with an air of seriousness owed largely to his slight stoop. "Allow half an hour for questions, and even then there should be nearly an hour before the concert."

"We should miss tea," Tess said, some conflict making itself felt within her bosom, "and I have hardly had a moment to speak to my mother or to Tamsin. Nor has Jude."

"I don't mind. It is only just over a fortnight to the end of term."

"Then shall we all come back here at four?" Tim said. "That would give you a break, Tess, and time to be with your family, and we could do all the really difficult bits."

"We haven't done the variations at all yet," Jude said.

"There is just time before lunch. Mr. Pinnegar, shall we try the last movement now?"

Owen pulled himself back with a great effort from the peace that had enclosed him : he had heard their voices, but not their words. The scene before him was very slightly blurred, an effect he put down to the shimmering noonday heat; as he tried also to believe that the continuous faint hum in his ears came from the bees in the ivy outside the window.

"The last movement, did you say? I played that through last night. It is not so difficult."

"Keep it a little slower than usual, Jude. It is allegretto, not allegro, remember; if we hurry the opening statement, you will be in trouble in the first variation."

He was not in trouble; the gasping leaps, the prodigious plunges up or down a couple of octaves were controlled and comfortable. Owen could not really listen to his son, he had some tricky bowing to bring off, but when the clarinet fell silent and he carried alone the calmer burden of the second variation he could feel as an acute loss the gap between his own accurate painstaking performance and the boy's inspired one : to hear the clarinet return above him in the later bars was to draw strength and purpose from the presence of a finished musician.

"Good, oh good!" Tim cried, and clapped his hands. "Very

good, everybody; the chromatic scale was perfect, Mr. Pinnegar. Now, Tess."

The viola variation went easily; Tess played modestly but well enough. Confidence mounted in them, almost perceptible as a distinct glow of warm feeling, to be dissipated painfully by a general display of ineptitude in the fourth variation, where racing semiquavers defeated Owen as completely at the second attempt as the first. Tim wrote something in his notebook, Tess just glanced at Jude, who got up and said roughly,

"That settles it."

"Sit down, Jude," Tim said at once, in a voice he rarely found it necessary to use.

"What's the good?" Jude said, and remained standing. "Why waste any more time?"

"There is still the adagio section to play."

"Play it by yourselves then. I've had enough."

"If we can take a few minutes to rest," Owen said, "I will try again : should anybody mind if we made it just a little slower?"

"I mind," Jude said at once. "Either we play it at the tempo Mozart asked for, or we don't play it at all."

Tim, who had witnessed exactly this scene not twenty-four hours before, with only one difference in the cast, thought he could not suffer the repetition to go any further : Jude must not be allowed to turn upon his own father the full force of his contempt and rage. He got up and signalled to Tess.

"Tess, I am sure your father would like a break now. Ian, go and get your lunch : I shall need you to help me later on."

When Ian had gone and Tess had taken Owen away, he said to Jude in a flat, hard tone,

"I hope you are proud of what you are doing?"

"I should be ashamed if I didn't do it," Jude said at once.

"People do not pay to come to our concert, Jude. The standard is higher than anyone has a right to expect."

"You said all this yesterday. You know what I said. It is no good going over it all again."

"There is a difference. Your father is here now."

"Yes, and he plays better than Daniel. But it is still not good enough."

"I suppose it is something," Tim said unwillingly," that you don't wish to shine by contrast."

"Don't you understand anything?" Jude now broke out, in a voice of desolation. "If Ian tears up a drawing or smashes a pot because he thinks it's no good, nobody calls him selfish."

"What he does hurts nobody but himself : you have made your father and Tess wretched, you know what you did to Daniel. It is not the same, you know it isn't."

"No, it is not the same at all," Jude said, and turned away to put his clarinet back in its case with fumbling hands. Tim could not look at him : when Celia came in a moment later she glanced from one to the other in painful indecision. One of these two surely required consolation, that much was clear; and even while she hesitated Jude rushed past her and out of the room.

"Oh, Tim ! Not another scene?"

"I think the scene was just averted, but it was a very near thing."

"The practice went badly?"

"It went far better than I would have dared hope, but fell a long way short of Jude's requirements."

"Oh, Tim !" she said again, on a little intake of breath. "Mr. Pinnegar is such a dear and he looks tired and worried : Jude should have a little more sense."

"It is not sense he lacks. You are right about Mr. Pinnegar; I think he may be ill."

"Will you have to cancel the concert?" she cried, as if that might be the end of all things.

"Perhaps. Clearly Jude thinks we should. It is my fault : I should have known the quintet was beyond us. Three piano solos and a handful of partsongs from the choir would have pleased the parents just as well."

"It isn't too late, even now, surely?"

"No, it is not too late," Tim said, with a sudden and total sense of collapse. "But I don't feel like doing it, I don't feel like sacrificing my work and Ian's and all that Tess has done."

"Come and have lunch. You will feel better afterwards."

"I am not hungry : it is too hot. Shall I drive you down to the village for a pint of bitter?"

"I don't like bitter, and we are needed here."

"Have you ever done anything you shouldn't, Celia? Have you ever, just once in your life, behaved really badly?"

"I am always falling short of my ideals," Celia said.

"I am not sure that that doesn't make it worse," he told her. "Being so good, and thinking you should be still better, it sounds as if you are in the grip of spiritual pride."

"Why are you never serious for two minutes together?" she said in a plaintive tone.

"Because you are serious enough for two," he said, regaining his good humour at a bound; he never lost it for long at a time, a fact well known by his more recalcitrant pupils, and even counted on to some extent by Jude.

The mouse was not upon the table; the box Clare had found for it was under Robert's chair. There were very few children in the dining room, most had gone off to lunch at the hotel, or even in Cardigan. Some were picnicking in the grounds. Meg put ham and salad on a plate for Clare.

"Do you like salad, Robert?"

"Not much. I don't mind tomatoes, if they are not squashy."

"These are good ones. Potato?"

"Has it got butter on it?"

"Try it and see," Meg said.

"It will be marge," said her daughter. "Butter on Sundays, or the fees would go up."

"No potato, thank you," Robert said politely.

"Is your father a doctor?" Clare said.

"He is an important sort of doctor called a surgeon."

"My mother was nearly a sort of doctor once."

"What about your father?"

"I don't know what he was. Mummy didn't know him very well. She doesn't like to talk about him."

Robert glanced at Meg under his eyelashes.

"My father says it is easy enough to buy a wedding ring. He said that in the car coming down, but your mother hasn't got one, so it cannot be so easy. And he said she would be called Mrs. Lindsay, but my mother said she would be Meg or Margaret, and she was right. My mother is very often right, but my father must be cleverer or he would not go to Denmark and places to show other people how to do things."

"Not everybody has wedding rings," Clare said. "Mummy doesn't wear jewellery: she doesn't like it. When there are free rings and necklaces in my comic she won't let me wear them."

"When are you two going to stop talking and start eating?" Meg said, coolly enough.

"It is too hot to eat," Clare said, with a pout of distaste, and pushed her plate away.

"There is ice cream for pudding."

"That is not meant to be a treat," Clare said kindly. "It is only because the Spaniards were too busy to make anything."

By half past one the meal was over.

"Come and lie down for a little while, Clare, "Meg said. "Would you like to rest too, Robert, until your parents come back?"

"I don't rest in the afternoon. I haven't since I was a little boy."

"I don't either," Clare said quickly.

"You sometimes lie on your bed with a book for a bit when it is hot, and there is nothing much to do. Perhaps we could find a book for Robert."

"Can the mouse come with us?"

"Yes, if you promise not to let him get out."

"It might be all right here," Robert said in a nonchalant tone, bending down to recover the box from beneath his chair.

"Hello, Mrs. Pinnegar! Pinnegar, hello!"

Helen smiled and waved her hand at Vincent; Owen neither heard nor saw him, scurrying to their table in a corner of the hotel dining room as to a place of refuge. Their children followed him, Helen bringing up the rear with Diggory. An altercation followed: Tamsin wished to sit between her brothers but this could not be arranged without Owen changing his seat, and Helen would not let him, though he was willing enough to do anything to keep the peace. Vincent watched everything with amusement, and Mrs. Daintry with other feelings.

"That is a lovely family, Harry," Emma said. "When I see them all together like that I wish that we could have had three or four."

"I wish I had even one," Dinah said, bringing a blush to the other woman's cheek as she realised her failure of tact. "Of course it is not too late to hope, I am only twenty-seven; who knows, I may have twenty more years of active reproductive life before me."

"Speak for yourself," Vincent said in a tender roar.

"Perhaps we should do something about it, see a doctor or something. Do you know anybody in the fertility line, Professor Branksome?"

"No," Harry said. After a moment he added, "I do not see much of the gynaecologists."

"Is that what I want, a gynaecologist? Or would one of the hormone people be better? Of course it might be Vincent, after all this time. We think not, because of Daniel, but things could alter in seventeen years."

Mrs. Daintry looked her son-in-law's wife up and down, and transferred her gaze to the Pinnegars as being, at least for the present, less offensive.

"There is always the element of risk," Dinah said, biting into her roll with beautiful teeth, whiter even than the bread they tore at. "Dan might not like a step-brother or sister; it might be difficult to treat them exactly alike."

"It might be impossible," Harry said, "when one would be in napkins and the other old enough to shave."

Vincent roared again, and everyone in the dining room looked round: Jude looked round with the rest and caught Mrs. Daintry's indignation full in the face.

"There he is, Vincent, there is the boy who bullies and persecutes your son. As soon as our meal is finished I think you should have a word with him, in front of his parents. They have the pleasure of their children's company and we have nothing."

"We have the Branksomes, Muriel," Dinah said, "and Vincent would not like to leave our guests."

The Branksomes saw that Vincent was indeed glad of their presence, and neither said a word.

"Well, if you will not speak to him, I will," Mrs. Daintry said and rose from her chair with a stiff movement that was pitiable, as nothing else about her was.

"Mother, no! I absolutely forbid it. You cannot intend to make a scene in a public place."

But this was Muriel's intention.

"What is it? What does she want?" Jude cried, as the old lady advanced upon him.

"Leave it to me," Tess said, putting a hand upon his arm. To the other guests, their encounter appeared, after all, a charming one; the elderly woman with her frail looks and flowery clothes exchanging a few words with a young girl; the girl's brother on his feet, apparently for politeness, though actually for flight. Nobody heard what passed between them except the three involved. "If you say a word to Jude," Tess said with gentle clarity, "I shall tell Daniel and he will not forgive you. If you leave us alone now, I will bring Daniel to you later in the afternoon."

"Your brother has nothing to fear from me," Muriel said, lowering her voice to match the girl's. "I should think his conscience would be harder on him than I am likely to be, knowing young boys as I do."

Jude might have spoken, but Tess's fingers digging into his arm kept him silent : and Muriel said no more, for Vincent now led her back to their table, smiling to right and left as he went.

"I hope you are satisfied. I hope you achieved whatever it was you set out to do, besides embarrassing Dinah and myself and our new friends."

"Yes, I am quite satisfied, dear," Muriel said, seating herself with the utmost composure, "and I consider that I have achieved something, since it is now quite clear to me that the Pinnegar girl is playing some deep game, perhaps on behalf of her brother. Things go on at that school, Vincent, that the censor would hardly allow if you were to write about them."

"Things go on everywhere," Dinah said, "and the censor has nothing to do with it."

"It is the age we live in," Muriel said, "if we can be said to live in it at all : I sometimes feel as if I had been dead a long time. So much happens and I am left out of it, I do not matter to anyone."

Her voice faltered, in reaction from her heroic confrontation of the terrifying young; it was her misfortune to get no credit for her heroism, when her courage was really equal to almost anything, was even equal to facing the hideous truth that Tess might have some grounds for her belief that Daniel would do for her what he could not rise to for love of his family.

"What did Daniel's grandmother want?" Helen asked in an unsuspicious tone when her two elder children sat down again, but showed no inclination to resume their meal.

"She thought I might know where Daniel is," Tess said.

"I thought it was Jude she was looking at, when she came over."

"Well, Jude might have known."

Helen was satisfied, her mild interest in Mrs. Daintry required no more than her children's casual tone and barely truthful words : Diggory was harder to please.

"Do you?"

"Do I what?" Tess said, turning her limpid eyes upon him.

"Know where Daniel is. Does Jude know?"

"It is none of your business," Jude said immediately : his sister's frown of warning came a moment too late.

"Would you like to finish my pudding, Diggory? I have had all I want."

"Tess must be sickening for something," Diggory said, accepting the bribe in the spirit in which it was offered.

"It is your favourite, Tess, too!" Tamsin said.

"It used to be," Tess corrected her. "People do not go on liking the same things for ever."

"I shall still like chocolate mousse when I am a hundred and ten," Tamsin said with conviction.

"Daniel's grandmother likes chocolate mousse," Diggory said, allowing his eyes to leave his plate for a moment, "and she must be a hundred and ten nearly."

"Oh, Diggory, what nonsense!" his mother cried. "She is about seventy, I would guess. What would you say, Owen?"

"Whatever you say, Helen. You are always good at telling people's ages."

"Does she live with the Hardys, I wonder?" Helen said, really wondering.

"Yes," Tess said. "When Daniel was little she looked after him; that was before his father married again."

"Of course they could not turn her out," Helen said.

"Some people would have," her husband suggested.

"I would have," Jude said under his breath.

"Mrs. Hardy must be a very sweet girl, to manage such a difficult situation," Helen said. "Most women would find it hard enough coping with a step-son, let alone a step-mother-in-law, or whatever the name would be."

Tess said with sudden vehemence, "It would be like having an old witch living with you."

"Hush, Tess," her mother said, though Tess had hardly spoken above a whisper. "What a thing to say! It is very sad for her, to have lost her daughter."

"It is very sad for Daniel not to have a mother, and he is not horrible and angry all the time."

"My dear, when has Mrs. Daintry been horrible? What can you have said to make her angry?"

"It would not matter what I said. She is angry because she is old and we are not."

"Some people do find that hard to bear," Owen said.

"Matthew says the Victorians thought all little children were as good as angels," Diggory said, "and that was why they kept on beating them, because they were always being disappointed."

"What has that got to do with it?" Tess said, peevishly, for her.

"People expect old people to be nice all the time now," Diggory said. "Of course we cannot beat them, we would not be allowed."

"I shall never be old," Jude said. "All the worthwhile people die early. Look at Mozart, and Schubert."

"And Mendelssohn and Schumann," his mother said eagerly.

"They were no loss."

"Keats," Tess said, "Shelley, Marlowe, Florence's Lawrence. It isn't only composers."

"If Daniel threw himself in the Teifi last night everyone would shake their heads sadly and talk about what he might have done if he had lived to a ripe old age," Diggory said, his cheerfulness seeming to augment at the thought of a friend cut off in early youth. "It would be almost worth being dead, if everyone thought that."

"Nobody drowns in the Teifi," Tess said, catching sight of her mother's face. "It is too shallow, especially now when the weather has been so dry."

Diggory said ruthlessly, "He could drown if he lay down flat and kept his head under, even when he began to feel as if his lungs would burst."

"Shut up, Diggory," Jude said. "His family is listening to you, the old lady might come back and eat you. I wouldn't stop her."

"She would get a jolly good meal," Diggory said in a complacent tone. "All my muscles and fat and offal and grapefruit and roast lamb and chocolate mousse; and cheese and biscuits too, if Mum says I may?"

"I suppose you may. Owen, is that our waitress, do you know?"

She was their waitress, and brought Diggory what he wanted, as well as coffee for his parents and a lemonade for Tamsin.

"You are very quiet, Tamsin," Helen said.

"It is too hot to talk much, and there is no time for me to talk, everyone else says so much so fast."

"Diggory, take her out with you while we go to the meeting, will you? Matthew never speaks for long, and she would like it so much."

"She could go with Tess," Diggory said. "Girls have things they talk about together."

"I shall be busy," Tess said at once. "I am sorry, Tamsin."

"Oh, well, I suppose I could stand her company for an hour."

"I will sit in the car," Tamsin said in a small voice.

"On such a hot day? No, dear, you go with Diggory, and get all the fresh air you can. And, Diggory, you are to be nice to her."

"Diggory does not know the meaning of the word nice," Jude said. "I would not like to tell you what Sam Trousdell told me this morning about your little boy."

"It is your fault he had anything to tell," Diggory said with furious indignation, and subsided as Tess kicked him under the table.

"I hope you have not been unkind to a smaller boy, Diggory?" Helen said.

"I wasn't half as unkind to him as Jude is to me," her younger son said as his resentment came to the boil.

"Why do people get nastier as they get older?" Tamsin said. "Diggory is beastly to Sam and Jude is beastly to Diggory and that old lady was horrid to Tess."

"Some people get nicer," Tess said. "Mum and Dad get nicer all the time."

"No, they don't," Tamsin said, only to herself.

"I shall probably get nicer," Diggory said.

"There is certainly room for improvement," Jude said with a laugh that was not perfectly kind.

"I hate to think what you will be like when you are seventy!" Tess said, with a flare of real temper.

"Tess, Tess! Jude was only joking: Diggory's feelings are not hurt."

"Only because I have none," Diggory said, and spread more butter on another biscuit.

"I shall never be seventy," Jude said, returning to an earlier topic that had made more of an impression on him than Tamsin's prospects for the afternoon, or Daniel's possible demise, or any question of Diggory's mellowing with age. "I shall go away somewhere and do myself in when I am about fifty-five. That way I shall not live to be a burden to my children."

"Let me know a few days beforehand," Diggory said, "and I will come and help you."

"You are both talking nonsense," Helen said in so hollow a tone that her boys fell silent at once. "You will not talk about serious things so lightly when you are a little older. Tess, will you find our waitress and ask for the bill?"

"I haven't finished my biscuit," Diggory said, "and there is still some butter on the dish."

"Hurry, then, we must not be late for Matthew."

"What upset Mum?" Tess said to Jude as they waited by the car for their parents to join them.

"Was she upset? I didn't notice."

"Yes, you did. Even Diggory did."

"She hates hot weather," Jude said, advancing physical discomfort as an acceptable reason for strange behaviour, since any other explanation might suggest that he had been the cause of it.

"I am sure something is the matter," Tess said. "Tamsin is playing up too; when she thinks nobody is watching she looks as if she wants to cry."

"Diggory will worm any secrets out of her," Jude said. "He is not too old to twist her arm if he thinks she is keeping anything to herself."

"You don't think he would, not really?"

"Keep her with you, if you are worried."

"I can't," Tess said, with a little moan for all the separate cares besetting her. "I have something else I must do."

"Oh, yes," Jude said, climbing into the back of the car as Owen and Helen came out of the hotel. "You have to see Daniel and tell him his dear old granny wants to see him. Do you think he will come back to please her?"

"He might, to please me," Tess said.

XI

IN THE EVENT Matthew's speech lasted less than half an hour. He gave a brief account of the main events of the year; a carol concert, a play, Sports Day : he touched upon certain recurrent problems of staffing, especially on the domestic side, and on the need for a new piano, since the pedals of the old one had fallen off during a recent recital. He mentioned plans for a new boiler and an extra bathroom for the younger children, and went in some detail into the progress of old pupils at university or in jobs.

Emma attended like the conscientious woman she was, and since she had taught in a boarding school herself she was able to recognise some of Cilrheddyn's problems and achievements as old ones shared by herself and her colleagues. After the speech, there were questions, a sort of discussion developed : some parents were concerned about their children's diet, or clothing, or hairstyles. Others wanted to know how various subjects were being taught, and whether full advantage were being taken of such aids as television or film strips or tape recordings. Matthew, or sometimes Janet, or sometimes one or other of the younger teachers answered the questions, advanced or defended various points of view. It was not so very different from other parents' meetings Emma had attended in her other capacity. Soon she became aware that it was hot, too hot for comfort, even with all the windows of the assembly hall wide open. Harry's eyes had been closed for some time; she was sure he was not asleep, was only giving his entire and critical attention to everything he heard. "Of course he is right to be critical," she told herself, "Sending Robert here would be a very big step to take; it is not to be decided all in a moment."

On her other side sat Mrs. Daintry, who was really asleep, her soft little cheeks blowing gently in and out with each tranquil breath, her lips occasionally separating with a tiny plop that almost woke her, roused her at least to the point of shaking her head a little, or looking around to remind herself of where she was and how little she liked it.

"This was the ballroom," she had said to Emma as they took their places on cheap stacking chairs. "Look at the floor; could anything be more shameful?" But a moment later she said, with faint regret that anything should surprise by pleasing her, "How lovely the flowers are! Janet Storace knows all there is to be known about growing things."

Beyond Mrs. Daintry sat Dinah, who asked several questions and made many chirping comments, all well to the point : beyond her again her husband, withdrawn in a reverie that Emma supposed must contain the image of his lost son. The sight of him reminded her that her own son was, for the moment, just as lost. She had passed Meg in the courtyard. "Robert is asleep on my bed," Meg said. "Clare has worn him out. If they wake up before the meeting is over she will take him out to play. I will see he comes to no harm." She went off before they could thank her, she was very busy.

"The child will have her mother's gift for making men fall in love with her," Harry said. "It is not just her looks either."

"I spoke to Miss Lindsay," Emma said. "I did have the chance, and I took it."

"That was good of you, Emma," Harry said in a tone of appreciation that struck his wife as disproportionate to the little effort she had made, or any satisfaction her approach could have given the younger woman. "What is wrong with me?" she asked herself now, twisting on her canvas chair to escape a sunbeam that sought her out as mercilessly as a searchlight, and made her eyes water. "Clearly I am jealous," she continued, while Celia spoke from the front row, turning round to confront the parents with her sweet severe face, protesting her faith in some forms of instruction, her scepticism about others. "It is not very clever of me to be jealous, nothing is likely to come of this meeting. If Harry feels a little interest in her, even a little tenderness, it will lead nowhere. I am not in any danger, Robert is not, and I am sure Miss Lindsay has other things to think of. The burned child does not play with fire."

"Yes, I know it is distressing," Matthew was now saying. "They are terrible pictures, all of us would rather the children had not seen them. All of us would rather such things did not happen and such photographs could not be taken. But this exhibition is not something any adult suggested : the children planned and carried it out themselves. And although I am horrified at what they have chosen, I am proud of them too. I hope you are proud, you should be. If they have been shocked into anger and compassion it is your doing as much as ours."

"All the same," Vincent said, as they walked out of the room side by side, "it doesn't help, do you think, to dwell on these matters? It isn't as if one does much good, simply by harping on the topic."

"And of course there is a morbid side to it," Dinah said, as if she had received her cue and was determined to deliver the right speech. "After a time people take a ghoulish pleasure in disasters, it all becomes tied up with perversions and pornography and the crudest type of sensationalism."

"And there is always the danger that by constantly reminding people of such beastliness they may actually get a little bored with it; people are a great deal more callous than one likes to think, and it is really only natural that they shouldn't wish to spend their time dwelling on that sort of thing."

Mrs. Daintry said, "What is everyone talking about? I must have missed something. My thoughts wandered a little, I daresay."

"The children made a sort of Chamber of Horrors, mother, awful photographs cut out of the newspapers."

"It does not surprise me. I suppose it had to come. Nothing is forbidden them, and nobody should be surprised at the result."

Vincent laughed loud and long.

"Mother dear, you have got hold of the wrong end of the stick as usual. The pictures were not obscene."

"Yes, they were," Harry said in a dangerous tone. "Mutilation is obscene. I should know. I have mutilated people."

He walked away from the Hardys, across the lawn; Emma said apprehensively,

"My husband feels strongly about this, Mr. Hardy."

"I could see that," Vincent said, in a tone of appealing ruefulness.

"He does not hide his feelings," Mrs. Daintry said. "We could all see how strongly he felt."

"I thought he was splendid!" Dinah said, her eyes aglow. "Vincent, I think I see a perfectly marvellous new story-line; I mean, why shouldn't our children do this sort of thing, organise an exhibition like this? Some of the parents would object, and somebody on the staff, a new science teacher, perhaps, just to show we all realise science itself is not to blame, could support them. It would be good for six or seven episodes at the very least."

"It would be useless, even for one."

"Oh, Vincent, why ever? We could build up a really tremendous clash of personalities; you know, all those songs the teenagers sing about the eve of destruction, and their parents and the older teachers simply hating it."

"The audience would simply hate it too. Not that it would ever get to the point of having an audience. George B. would put his foot down before you even got a page of it duplicated. It is completely unsuitable for a show that goes out in the early evening. Everything we do must be fit for family viewing."

"But, Vincent, we wouldn't actually show any of those awful pictures, we could just imply them. It could all be kept in perfectly good taste."

They walked away, happily deep in discussion: Emma found herself alone with Mrs. Daintry.

"I see your little boy has deserted you," Mrs. Daintry said.

"Yes, he was asleep when the meeting started. I must really start to search for him now."

"You should spare yourself the trouble; it is too hot for searching, and he might be anywhere. When he is hungry he will come back."

"All the same, I ought to find Miss Lindsay. It is not fair that she should have the worry of looking after him when she has so many other things to do."

When Emma had excused herself and wandered rather uncertainly towards the swimming pool, Muriel chose to sit on a wooden bench that encircled the massive trunk of a chestnut tree.

"They all go off: nobody considers that I might be lonely. Sitting here on my own I might have a seizure and never be able to speak again. They would come back with their smiling faces, and at first they would joke about my falling asleep with my mouth open. But soon they would realise that something was wrong : I would be taken to hospital and nursed with great care. They would be very sorry, certainly Dinah would, she is a good kind girl, though frequently I find her rather irritating."

Her thoughts dwelt for some time comfortably on the discomfiture of her connections, more comfortably still on Daniel's grief when he should discover how he had denied her the pleasure of his company during her last conscious hours, less comfortably by far on what might follow, perhaps years later, perhaps only months, weeks, days later : the thankful recognition on all those others' parts of a problem solved for ever, a burden shed.

"You will not come to any harm while you are with me," Clare said. "I am considered very reliable for my age."

"My people will not know where I am. Mummy might be worried."

"The parents' meeting goes on for hours and hours. You know how they talk. We shall be back before it is over."

"All the same I would rather stay here."

"If you come with me, you may keep the mouse."

"Really keep it? For good?"

"I have plenty. It will be nice to know he has a good home."

"He won't have," Robert said, returning sadly to the realities of the situation. "They would never let me keep a mouse."

"Has your car got a boot?" Clare said.

"Of course it has. All cars have boots, don't they?"

"No, some foreign ones have engines. But if yours is the usual kind we could hide the box in it now, and you would go off home and they wouldn't find out. You could smuggle it up to your room and steal out at dead of night to find crumbs for it. Have you got any money?"

"I think I have. Why?"

"You would have to buy a cage, a mouse can nibble its way out of a cardboard box quick as a wink. Do they let you go out by yourself when you are at home?"

"Of course they do!" Robert cried with splendid indignation, though in fact he rarely left the house alone and never without explaining his purposes.

"Then first thing on Monday morning you must go to a pet shop and buy a cage, even if you are late for school. You could buy some food too, in case you are scared of going downstairs after dark."

"I am not scared of the dark."

"I thought you might be," she said, very casually, "since you are scared of coming with me now."

"Who says I'm scared?"

She gave him the box with the mouse in it.

"Come on, then : we will hide him on the way."

Harry had not thought it necessary to lock the boot; these children were able to carry out their plan with ease. They stood looking at each other, both breathing a little faster than usual, in spite of Clare's nonchalance.

"What are you two up to?" Meg said. "Would you like a cup of tea? I am just going over to see if Florence will make me one."

"I don't want any tea, thank you," Clare said politely. "Robert doesn't want any either. May we go for a walk?"

"Yes, if you have your watch on. You must be back by four so that the Branksomes can get away if they want to. I don't think they are staying to the concert."

"Come on, Robert."

He went after her as if she had him on a lead. Meg smiled, and then frowned. Something in her daughter's accomplished handling of the little boy aroused a faint distaste in her. She turned with relief to Florence who would never wield such power, though she was quite a pretty girl, and a clever one, and tender-hearted too.

"Tell Nancy to come and have a cup while she can," Meg said. "She must be fed up, sitting at that stall all day. I thought Kate was to take over?"

"Kate is playing tennis with Peter," Florence said. "She is coming along afterwards, at least she said she would."

"She will go swimming with Peter," Nancy said, taking a cup of tea with an air of thankfulness. "I shall not see her again this afternoon."

"It is really too bad!"

"No, it is exactly as bad as it would be," Nancy said. "Expecting Kate to be any different would be self deception, or false optimism, or something. When we have finished our tea, Flo, we must start bringing out the cakes and the strawberries. Meg! Is the cream in the fridge?"

"I expect so," Meg said with a gentle yawn. "It had better stay there till the very last moment. I don't believe it could be hotter in Egypt than it is in this courtyard at the moment."

"Why don't you have a swim, Meg?"

"I more or less promised to keep an eye on that little boy. If Clare pushes him over or jumps on him I must be around to apologise for her."

Even to her own ears this sounded lame : the swimming pool was not so far away that to dive into the cool water would be irresponsible, the real reason for her reluctance to go and change was so unlikely that when she allowed her thoughts to dwell on it for a moment she had to suppress a laugh. To want to see Harry Branksome again, when he had practically cut her in the morning; to hope to exchange a few words with him when there was nothing they could talk about except his child, or his wife, all other topics of mutual interest being unmentionable! The laugh would not be suppressed, it welled up beautifully, she threw her head back and gave way to it. Florence and Nancy had taken the cups away to wash, there was no one to hear her. When she became quiet again she decided to swim in defiance of her own idiocy; this seemed to her even a moral decision. She took some care not to ask herself why.

"I would not eat that blade of grass if I were you," Diggory said. "Consider what has nourished it."

Tamsin dropped the grass as if it were electrified, and squealed rather less loudly than Diggory had intended.

"All these dead Evanses and Joneses and Llewellyns and Powells keep the grass and the nettles and the bindweed going," he said, hoping for another squeal, but Tamsin disappointed him, sitting down suddenly upon the gravestone Daniel had cleared and pushing that boy's jar of honeysuckle to one side without looking at it. Tears glistened on her cheeks and the cheeks were pale.

"Did I upset you?" Diggory asked, planting himself foursquare in front of his sister with an expression of genuine interest.

"No, it is not anything you said."

"If you are going to howl I shall go away and leave you.

You will be alone among the tombs and their grisly contents."

"I don't care about the tombs," Tamsin said : her tears fell thick and fast; she had no handkerchief and put her arm up to her face to wipe her eyes on her attenuated sleeve. Last year's dress was tight across her shoulders and tore, and it seemed as if there would be no end to her sobbing.

"You can have my handkerchief," Diggory said, and shook sand, stones and toffee wrappings out of the piece of cloth he handed her; but she would not take it.

"I am going, Tamsin. I warned you."

For answer she turned and leant her brow against the head-stone. Diggory walked away with his head down, kicking at nettles. At the wicket gate he looked back; she had not stirred. "Goodbye," he called. "Now I know what crying fit to wake the dead sounds like."

Tamsin opened her heavy eyes to see what dead she would be waking; the lettering on the headstone had never been deeply cut, for this was cheapish work, done at the parish's expense. She could not decipher the name, and the date was in Roman numerals, far too many of them for her meagre knowledge. The figure nine was clear, a closer look showed that it came in the middle of a sentence; in the ninth year of his age someone had died. "Nobody dies before they are a hundred these days," her mother had told her not long ago when they had seen a cat run over in the road. "I certainly don't mean to. I want to be here to help you look after your children, and even your children's children."

"It is not true," Tamsin said now; she had known perfectly well that it was not true at the time, but had understood that to believe it would be best for her and for her mother. But she was not to come to Cilrheddyn, any more than she was to live to be a hundred, she felt it in her bones. Her father would never, she was perfectly certain he would never, dash down her hopes without cause; why she should be so sure of this one thing when all her other certainties were failing her she did not know, or care. Children of her own age could die and be buried and help the grass to grow. She sat on the warm indifferent stone and wept. Presently a shadow fell across her.

"I found a snail," Diggory said, "the kind you like, with stripes on. If you want I will find another and we will race them. This thing you are sitting on would make a good track."

"It never works. They go a few inches and then change their minds and go off after food."

"We would pick fresh leaves and tempt them, like carrots in front of donkeys."

She scrambled up.

"Where did you find it?"

"On that stuff with yellow leaves under the hedge."

They had found a second snail and were back at the child's grave when Clare and Robert reached the wicket gate.

"Somebody is here before us," Clare said.

"I want to go back. I don't like this place : if I had known where you were taking me I wouldn't have come."

"It is only Diggory and his silly sister. If she is not afraid I don't see why you should be."

"What is the time?" Robert asked in a hoarse tone of despair.

"Only twenty past three," Clare said without a glance at her watch. "It will only take us ten minutes to get back so there is no hurry."

"I am going back now."

"All right. Go back alone if you want to. I daresay my mother will hit me when she finds I have let you go off by yourself."

"Does she hit you?"

"She hits me and shouts at me like a mad woman," Clare said, studying Robert's face dispassionately.

"My mother would never do that."

"I expect she would get your father to do it."

"My father is away all day. Often I am in bed when he comes home at night. My mother says she will tell him how naughty I have been but I don't believe she does, she thinks it is wrong to worry him when he is tired."

"Sometimes I wish I had a father, as more ordinary children do."

"It is not anything special," Robert said. "Only two people to go on at you instead of one."

"Diggory!" Clare called. "What are you doing?"

"Racing snails. If you can find one you can join in. Tamsin's hasn't crossed the starting line yet."

Clare and Robert found snails and knelt by the gravestone.

Such a crowd was sure to end in clumsiness; it was Clare who knocked over the jamjar. The snails' horns and then their heads went in as the stream of water reached them.

"Blast," Diggory said. "Mine was winning."

"It would have been a walk over," Tamsin said.

"A slither over," Robert said, hardly aloud. The other children looked at him, considering whether to laugh. Diggory finally laughed and the girls followed suit. Robert followed up his advantage.

"Who put the silly jar there anyway?"

"People do put flowers on graves," Clare said.

"Flowers put themselves on these graves," Diggory said, starting off another burst of laughter.

"There is one of these places almost next to my father's school," Tamsin said.

"They are called cemeteries," Diggory said.

"They are called graveyards," Clare said. "Sensible people are burned not buried, it takes up less room, my mother says."

"This one was burned and buried," Diggory said. "Rhys, something or other I can't read, in the ninth year of his age, in the chimney in Cilrheddyn Great Hall."

There was a silence.

"Cilrheddyn Great Hall, isn't that our school?" Clare said in a light voice, keeping her eyes off Diggory.

"Of course it is. Are you coming to Cilrheddyn?" he said to Robert.

"No, I don't think so. I am almost sure not."

"Pity," Diggory said casually. "We don't push little boys up the chimneys these days, in case you were worrying."

"Do you suppose he was a sweep?" Tamsin said, her tears springing afresh.

"What else? Even a hundred years ago children didn't climb chimneys just for the fun of it."

"How do you know it was a hundred years ago?" Robert asked.

"Can't you read?"

"There aren't any numbers on the stone to make a date."

"There are special numbers that look like letters," Diggory said kindly. "The Arabs invented proper ones, the Romans had to make do with C's and V's and X's."

"Romans would not have been here only a hundred years

ago," Robert said, looking around him as if they might be here, now, this very day. "Romans did not need chimney sweeps," he went on, displaying a breadth of knowledge that would have astounded his father, "they had central heating."

"It is not much good talking to you," Diggory said. "You want to do all the talking yourself."

Robert fell silent.

"The Welsh," Diggory said, now that he was master of his audience, "are very keen on grammar schools and exams and that sort of thing so naturally they use Latin on their tombstones."

"It is all English," Clare said, "except the C's and V's and things."

"Latin and English are both foreign languages in Pembrokeshire, so you can see how the Welsh go in for education. When they have been educated themselves they go all over the place teaching other people."

"I know some Welsh," Clare said. "At my school we all speak it in the play-yard."

"Speak some now," Tamsin said.

Clare said half a dozen words, which might have been Welsh: before she could be asked for any further demonstration Tess came through the wicket gate. She stopped at the sight of them.

"Whatever are you doing here, Diggory? Take Tamsin back at once!"

"We are not doing any harm. We are not in anyone's way. Nobody minded our being here until you came."

The children stood in a row, turning angry faces to the big girl; Clare took Robert's hand reassuringly. His palm and hers stuck together from heat and fear and indignation.

"What have you got there?" Tess said, coming nearer.

"Snails," Diggory said, continuing to be spokesman as of right. "We shall put them back when we have finished. They enjoy racing; it brings a little excitement into their humdrum lives."

"You should not play on a grave. It is the sort of thing people do not do."

"Snails are not people, and we are not on the grave, we are only round it."

"Diggory Pinnegar, there are times when I could wring your neck."

"Try it," Diggory said, sensing that the storm was past.

"Tea will be ready soon, and then the concert. You must be getting back in a little while."

"Why did you come down here?" Diggory asked with a sudden perception of possible causes. "Are you going to pray?"

"I am just going into the church for a few minutes," Tess said with what dignity she could muster, "and if you are not out of here by the time I come back I shall tell Mummy that you are not to have any strawberries."

"Take no notice," Diggory said comfortably when the door of the church had closed behind her. "Tess's bark is worse than her bite, and my mother does not even bark, she hardly whimpers."

One of the four snails had seized its chance, and made a bid for freedom; it was recaptured and lined up with the others, the ferocious sun had already dried the spilled water.

"Mine is the prettiest," Clare said. Nobody challenged her, for there could be no argument on the point; the rest of the snails were handsome with bold white bands on a background as brown and glossy as a chestnut, but Clare's was a beautiful pale greenish yellow, and its bands were hardly broader than a curl of pale blonde hair.

"I wonder if Tess has brought anything to eat?" Diggory said some time later when his own snail had advanced over an inch.

"Go and ask her. She usually has something in her pocket."

"She bulged," Robert said, and flushed under their triple gaze. "I don't know what she looks like usually, but I thought she had something stuffed into the front of her dress."

"Those were her breasts," Diggory said. "She is almost grown up."

Robert's flush intensified; he picked his snail off the gravestone and walked away with it.

"Now he is upset," Tamsin said. "You shouldn't have said that, Diggory. He has no sisters."

"He has a mother. He must have noticed."

"He is very easily upset," Clare said. "Leave him alone and he will get over it."

Their heads went down again; when Mrs. Daintry opened the wicket gate she saw just the three children.

"Where is the little boy you are supposed to be looking after?" she called to Clare; she had picked a switch out of the hedgerow as she came along and walked purposefully between the head-stones, laying the nettles low as she came.

"He is here: he is all right," Diggory said.

"I was not speaking to you, young man."

"I know you were not, but Clare is frightened, and I thought I should answer you. I expect you wanted an answer."

"Where is your sister?" Mrs. Daintry said, setting his impudence on one side for the moment. She could see Robert now, in the shade of an elder tree, facing away from her, but of Tess whom she had followed from the school garden there was no sign.

"My sister is here," Diggory said, getting up and pulling Tamsin to her feet. Mrs. Daintry's glance took in the child's face streaked with grime and dried tears, her torn dress and dishevelled hair.

"I meant your other sister."

"I don't think there is anyone else in the graveyard," Diggory said blandly, "except the dead."

"Has anybody ever told you that you are a rude little boy?"

"Yes," Diggory said.

"Perhaps a little girl would be more polite," Mrs. Daintry said, turning from Tamsin to Clare with an inviting smile, since blood is known to be thicker than water. "Clare, dear, have you seen this rude boy's big sister?"

"Yes, often," Clare said, rolling her head from side to side in a plausible imitation of idiocy.

"I know where she is," Robert said, coming away from the deep shadows. "She went into the church."

The bees hummed, the birds sang, but there was nevertheless a cold silence. Robert did not look at anybody; he turned and walked out of the churchyard.

"Thank you very much, Robert," Mrs. Daintry called after him, "I shall tell your mother what a helpful boy you have been."

"Will he get lost?" Tamsin said anxiously.

"I hope so," Diggory said.

"It is what boys like that would do," Clare said.

"He is younger than any of us," Tamsin said, in a reluctant voice.

"He is older than I am," Clare said. "I could find my way back from almost anywhere."

Tamsin said nothing but picked up her snail and put it carefully in a patch of dockleaves : then she went through the wicket gate. Mrs. Daintry stood by the church door; she had walked there very slowly, in deference to the heat, and her age, and the uncertainty of her purpose. Now she swayed slightly on her little feet in their well-polished shoes.

"Why doesn't she go in?" Clare said. "She knows Tess is there."

"Daniel is there too," Diggory said. "That is why Tess came."

"What are they doing in there? Why aren't they with everyone else eating strawberries?"

"Tess brought some food with her. Robert was right about the bulges."

"That old lady is Daniel's grannie," Clare said. "I expect she just wants to see him. Perhaps we shouldn't have tried to stop her."

"She can see Daniel whenever she wants to. It is Tess I wouldn't let her see. She hates Tess."

"It was no use being rude to her. She will do what she wants. We shall get into trouble, all for nothing."

Mrs. Daintry sat in the porch, waiting. The children came up to her. Diggory said, "Clare and I are sorry we were rude. If you like I will go in and tell my sister you are here."

"That is better," Mrs. Daintry said, "but there is no need. I shall just rest quietly for a minute and then go in myself." As Diggory's fingers closed on the handle of the inner door, she continued in a low tone that was charged with menace. "I forbid you to warn the pair of them. Do you understand me? Whatever it is they are up to, I mean to catch them at it."

"Here is Tamsin," Clare said, clutching Diggory's hand with an impulse of real terror, "and Robert and his father. Hide me, he will be so angry."

But Harry took no notice of Clare, cowering in the dark corner behind Diggory, except to say, "Is your sister in there?" and to accept the boy's silence as sufficient answer. Mrs. Daintry rose.

"You have come at just the right moment, Professor Branksome. I must say it, even though my grandson is involved. You could not have hoped for a better demonstration of what goes on here, of the sort of education you will be paying for."

Harry opened the church door. The place was as dark and

airless as a tomb. He could see nothing at first. He heard nothing until Tess whispered,

"Come in quietly, Diggory; don't make a sound. We are feeding a church mouse."

"It isn't Diggory," Harry said in his ordinary voice.

Her head sprang up over the back of the last pew on the right: so did Daniel's. Harry was not much good at reading faces but these had neither the flush of shame nor the pallor of real guilt.

"He will never come back now," Tess said in reproach. "You have scared him away. He was almost ready to eat from Daniel's hand."

"If you are Daniel," Harry said to the boy with a sense that it was his own confusion that needed covering, "your grandmother is outside, waiting for you. You should go to her now; it is far too hot for an old lady to be walking about alone."

Daniel looked at Tess who nodded and came out of the pew with an empty paper bag and some chocolate wrappings. Harry took in, almost as if he were loth to do so, the decent composure of her dress, her unruffled hair. In a tone more brusque than he intended he said to the girl, "It was you I came to find: your mother wants you." Then he added more gently, "There is nothing to be frightened of. It is just that your father is not feeling well."

XII

"I OUGHT TO BUY something off the cakestall," Emma had said to Harry not half an hour before. "Those little ginger biscuits look quite nice. Perhaps I can buy a tin or something in the village to keep them crisp on the way home."

"The tin or something will probably cost you more than the biscuits."

"Never mind, Robert has had a lovely day, I feel that is worth anything, even ginger biscuits at three shillings the pound."

"Where do you think he has got to?" Harry said, looking around.

"Miss Lindsay's little girl took him to see her secret place, Janet says. I expect it is a den in the woods or a tree house, Robert would love that. Miss Lindsay told her they were to be back by four."

"It is almost that now: can the child tell the time? Robert cannot, and she is younger than our boy."

"I suppose she would not have a watch if she could not. Robert can tell the hours and the half hours, Harry, if he is not rushed."

"Buy your biscuits, Emma, and I will just look round and see if they are anywhere about. I should like to get away fairly soon."

"Harry," Emma began: he was not looking at her, he was looking around the courtyard, where two small children might easily be hidden among so many larger ones and such a quantity of adults. "Harry," she said again, touching him gently on the sleeve, "should you mind very much if we stayed for the concert?"

"No, not very much," he said after a moment's hesitation. "Music means nothing to me, you know that, but I can sit through an hour of it, if it would please you. Robert will wriggle and fret, though, won't he?"

"I thought," she said, shamefaced, "that if he were still enjoying himself we might leave him with the other children."

"Or I could stay with him," Harry said, as if this were a thing a father would not ordinarily do. "There must be a cricket pitch somewhere, perhaps we could borrow a bat and a ball."

"Should you like that?" she said doubtfully.

"No," Harry admitted, "and nor would Robert. But we will find something, there is no need to worry. I could even drive him down to Newcastle Emlyn to find a tin for your biscuits."

"Oh, that is a good idea. I will get them now, at once."

But when she got back to Nancy's stall there were no biscuits left.

"There are rock cakes," Nancy said. "There generally are, when everything else has gone. There is some strawberry jam, but Susan thought she could use the strawberries that weren't good enough for the visitors and it will not set. It is quite nice as a sort of drink."

"I think it might make a mess in the car," Emma said tactfully. "I will have a dozen of the rock cakes, please."

"Are you sure?" Nancy said.

"I made those rock cakes," Kate said with hauteur. "Peter said they were very good."

"That proves nothing, except his devotion," Nancy said. "What have you done with the lad?"

"He is helping Ian and Jude arrange chairs in the music room. They sent me over to get some food."

"Rock cakes?"

"Well, no. Are there any of Sally's doughnuts?"

"There is only what you see. Peter's love is to be tested in the furnace."

"There is proper tea in the library for visitors," Kate told Emma, "with egg and cress sandwiches and little sausages on sticks."

"Thank you very much, we shall like that."

"We should like it too," Nancy said. "The cakes will be three shillings and sixpence, please."

"What have you got there?" Harry said when Emma joined him. "We shall need a very large tin for all those."

"I think they are rather past needing a tin, Harry. Robert could feed them to the ducks on the Round Stone Pond tomorrow. Shall we have some tea, or would you rather look for Robert?"

"We could do both; we could watch out for him on our way to the library."

Perhaps because she was searching for her child, Emma found something different.

"Just a moment, Harry : over there, look, something is happening. It is that grey man with all the children."

Owen had sunk on to a bench; his eyes were closed. Helen knelt beside him, his hands between her own. Children ran up with glasses of water, somebody brought a paper fan.

"He must be ill, Harry. Can you do anything?"

Harry swore under his breath and pushed his way to Owen's side.

"Can I help? I am a sort of doctor."

Helen looked up with dilated eyes, and Harry lifted her husband's wrist while he watched the immobile face, the drops of sweat breaking out above the eyebrows.

"It is his blood pressure," Helen said. "He is having treatment, he said earlier that his head ached and I took no special notice."

Nancy's father said in a gruff manner.

"Good afternoon, doctor; may I join you? I have the advantage of being an old acquaintance of Pinnegar's."

It was years since Harry had been called "Doctor," and nearly as long since anybody had dared offer him unasked-for assistance; but in these circumstances professional pride seemed of no importance.

"We will just improvise a stretcher," Nancy's father said, easily taking command of the situation, "and then we will get him out of the crowd and the sun and the heat. They cannot be doing him any good, eh, doctor?"

"I am sure you know much better than I what to do in an emergency like this," Harry said gracefully enough.

"It is so very common, all too common these days, professional men driving themselves too hard. Would you say your husband drove himself too hard, Mrs. Pinnegar?"

But Helen burst into tears, and Janet came up and helped her to her feet.

"Come inside, dear, we have a couch in Matron's office. Dr.

Spalding, would you bring Mr. Pinnegar along there? Peter and Ian have gone to fetch a camp-bed; it will make a stretcher of sorts."

Owen opened his eyes and half rose from the bench.

"Sit still," Dr. Spalding said in a crisp voice. "Do not attempt to stand up, Mr. Pinnegar. We will get you into the house in a few minutes."

"I can walk there," Owen said in a voice which was steady if weak. "The heat has made my head ache, that is all."

"No pain in your chest? No difficulty with your breathing?"

Owen shook his head; the movement hurt him, but his colour was improving moment by moment.

"I think I forgot to take my tablets at lunchtime," he said. "They are in my wife's handbag, should I take them now?"

"I would like to see them first," Dr. Spalding said, and to Harry, "I am sure you agree that that would be wise?"

"Yes," Harry said, "and it would also be wise to take Mr. Pinnegar to his wife now, so that she need not be in doubt any longer."

Owen got cautiously to his feet, resisting offers of aid with an impatient smile.

"We shall manage without that," Dr. Spalding said to Ian and Peter rushing up with a canvas daybed and looks of authority, so that people melted away on either side with low murmurs of respect. He offered Owen his arm, they went off together, and Harry rejoined Emma; Janet called from the doorway, "Peter, Ian, do either of you know where Tess is? Her mother wants her."

Nobody knew, heads shook all round and voices buzzed, producing a variety of suggestions.

"She will be back at four," Ian said, "we are supposed to fit in another rehearsal."

Janet withdrew into the house.

"Perhaps I should look for the children," Emma said.

"No," Harry said. "You go to the library and find a cup of tea. You look tired. I will find out where they have got to."

He made sure once again that they were not in the courtyard, walked round the outside of the buildings and met Meg on her way back from the pool, glistening wet, her hair clinging in dark streaks to her forehead. Her hand flew to her mouth.

"What has happened? Are they in any trouble?"

"Not that I know of," Harry said coolly. "Where would they be, Miss Lindsay? My wife fusses over Robert more than she should, I daresay."

Meg thought rapidly.

"They are not with the rabbits or I would have seen them; and Clare would not climb trees in her new dress, so I don't think they will be in the wood." She added, with reluctance, "There is another place they go to sometimes, a deserted church where the key hangs in the porch and some of the more daring children go in and play the organ. Clare might just have taken him there."

"Where is it?" Harry said.

"If you go out of the gates and up the road, there is a turning on the right, hardly any distance away. It is a proper lane to begin with, later on it gives up. There are a few old cottages. I should think you would hear them if they are down there."

He said abruptly, "I should not have stopped you, you will be getting chilled in your wet things."

Meg had scarcely been conscious of her bathing suit clinging to her; she had a towel in her hand, and with a swift movement drew it about her waist, looking down as she did so. When she spoke her voice was fully under control.

"Getting chilled on such a day is nothing to be afraid of. But thank you for thinking of it. I will go and dress."

She walked off. Harry made for the school gates and followed her directions. Before he reached the abandoned village he heard his son.

"This isn't the way I came. I don't remember those houses."

"Clare brought you through the woods then," Tamsin said. "This takes longer, but I don't know the other way very well."

"I am not going any further unless Clare comes. She was told to look after me."

"It was you who went off," Tamsin said. "You left Clare behind, it is no good blaming her."

"You are as bad as your brother," Robert now cried. "All of you are horrible. I shall tell my father not to send me here."

The children confronted each other in the middle of the dusty track, Tamsin rocking to and fro on her heels, arms akimbo.

Harry stayed where he was, under the neglected hedgerow, a little cloud of gnats hovering about him.

"Don't you want to come to Cilrheddyn?" Tamsin breathed.

"Not likely," Robert said, in bitterness of spirit.

"I wish I were you," she said, equally bitter. "I wish I didn't want to."

"What do you mean?" he said, sorting this out and making no sense of it.

"I was supposed to come in September, or after Christmas. I would have been with Tess and Diggory and all their friends."

"And now you aren't coming?"

"Daddy says perhaps not. And I am sure he means not possibly ever."

"Why not? Is he fed up with the place?"

"I expect it is the fees," Tamsin said. "We are not specially rich. You may be, if there is only one of you."

"Do people pay money to send their children here?"

"Of course they do," she said in scorn.

"Suppose I asked them not to send me, and to give the money to your father, so that he could pay for you to come?" Robert cried, his imagination carrying him at a bound over those difficulties within his comprehension; he was happily unaware of some greater difficulties beyond, but Tamsin was a year older, and in her mother's confidence.

"Grown-ups cannot take money from other grown-ups, even if they would like to. It would be kind of your father, but my father could not do it."

"Why not, if it made us both happy?"

"I don't know why not, I expect there is a law against it."

They walked on, discouraged, and Harry went to meet them. "Where is the other little girl, Robert?"

"She is still in the churchyard. There are lots of people there, the old lady from the hotel, and this one's brother, and another sister, who went into the church."

"The big girl called Tess?" Harry said quickly to Tamsin.

"Yes, how did you know?"

"Your mother wants her," Harry said. "Come back and help me find her."

"All right," Tamsin said, and took his hand. After they had gone a few steps Harry held out his other hand awkwardly to his son. They did not let go of each other until they reached the wicket gate.

"We have told the children nothing yet," Helen said. "We only knew how much there was to tell a few weeks ago."

"We may have to take Diggory away," Owen said, "but of course we will give you a term's notice. He can come back until Christmas anyhow. After that every penny will count."

Janet got up from her chair and walked over to the window.

"We have a small bursary fund, and there are other sources that might be tapped. I don't think you need worry about Diggory. Tess is all right, of course, and Jude has his scholarship now. Did your little girl think she was coming here?"

"She was sure of it," Owen said bleakly, "until last night, when I had a sort of presentiment and warned her that she should not take it for granted." He smiled at Helen in a shamefaced way but she only said,

"So that is why she has been difficult all day; I thought it was not just the heat and her old dress, Tamsin is not silly or selfish as a rule."

"None of your children is any of those things," Janet said with warmth.

"Sometimes I think that Jude is, not silly of course, but selfish," Helen said. "I know Owen thinks I spoil him, but it is hard to admire one's own child and still treat him as the child he really is."

"Yes, there is a danger that he may think a little too well of himself," Janet said, mildly in the circumstances. "It may be that your trouble will bring out qualities in him he has never needed to show until now."

"We would rather he did not know yet, at least until the concert is over."

"Helen, dear," Owen said, "how can there be a concert?"

"Poor Jude," Helen said, when she understood this.

"I will find Tim: Tim would be the best person to break it to him," Janet said. "And, please, Mrs. Pinnegar, try not to let Jude's disappointment add to your other worries. He will be disappointed, of course, but he has so much to look forward to. The blow will be sharp, but the pain will soon be over."

Tim was already in the music room when Janet went to find

him. He was arranging music on the stands : Celia sat in the shadows, seeming to watch him.

"There is bad news, Tim. Mr. Pinnegar was taken ill in the courtyard, and won't be able to play."

"Oh, hell," Tim said, uncharacteristically, but the heat was trying for him as for everyone else, and his bulk made it no easier to bear. He took out a handkerchief and wiped his hands and brow. "All that work and temper and embarrassment for nothing!"

"Embarrassment?" Janet said.

"Jude saw no reason to relax his standards for the sake of his father," Tim said. "I think Mr. Pinnegar is wise to give up : it was very fine of him even to try."

"He has no choice," Janet said. "He is a very sick man. He and his wife prefer that the children should not know before they have to : I only tell you now because it would be unfair to Mr. Pinnegar to let you believe that there in anything factitious in his condition. I trust you to keep it to yourself."

Celia stirred, but Janet did not look her way; when she left the room to return to Helen the younger woman got up.

"I will find Jude for you."

"Why bother? He will be here soon enough. They are all supposed to be here at four. Let him have his tea in peace; when I last saw him he was taking one of Florence's hot dogs out to his tent."

"It is strange that excitement does not affect their appetites. I have eaten nothing all day."

"Why, what are you excited about?"

"It is the heat that I find hard to stand," Celia said reprovingly.

"You look as cool as a folded leaf, and light enough to blow away if there were a puff of wind."

"What a pretty speech," she said, with genuine appreciation.

"Yes, I am quite proud of it : it would not do for Tess."

"That nasturtium colour does suit her, though, Tim, with her dark skin and hair. It is not what I would choose, but she has plenty of time to learn."

"Sheathe your claws," he said; it was his turn to administer a reproof, and hers to look away. "You know my caring for Tess does not matter a scrap to you. You should not begrudge me a legitimate interest in my pupil."

"So long as it is legitimate," she said, with a little flash of those claws : and with a transition that was less abrupt than it seemed, "Did I tell you that I was thinking of leaving at Christmas?"

"No, you didn't tell me. I thought you might be."

"The first year I was here I taught as I had been shown in college, everybody hated it : I began to hate it myself. The bigger ones found good reasons not to come to my lessons and the examination results were awful. I knew I was not to blame, nobody blamed me, but I felt awful. This year I tried something different, most of them liked it, though one or two perverse ones wanted conjugations and declensions and the use of the subjunctive every single period. I am pretty sure the results will be awful again."

"Matthew would say, look beyond the examination results, look at the young men and women themselves. You will have helped the ones with a natural aptitude, and you won't have made the others feel useless. Even the parents can see that, except in moments of panic when they really believe that a nine to five job and a sound banker's reference are the whole purpose of life."

"They are not such bad things, Tim. Nearly everyone settles for them in the end."

"As long as it is only nearly."

"I know Matthew is right, or I think he is," she said miserably, "but I was taught differently, and the teachers did their job too well. I never was a rebel, I only took this job because I wanted to work in the country and in a co-educational school. Janet knows that : she will not really be sorry to see me go."

"Shall you be sorry yourself, Celia?"

"Perhaps I will. I shall miss some of the children, and Meg, and you, of course, Tim."

"Am I too early?" Jude said finding them close together, and sensing that they had been closer still; he could not know that the kiss had been one of goodwill, not passion, and that Celia's recoil was not from the kiss itself, but from the meaning the boy might read into it.

"Not at all," Tim said in his blandest tone. "We were expecting you. I'm afraid I have bad news, Jude. Your father is ill, and we shall have to cancel the concert."

"Well, thank God for that!" Jude cried.

"Think what you are saying," Tim said.

Jude looked from one to the other with a sense of outrage; he could not account for the revulsion in their faces.

"He looked rotten at lunchtime. The heat has got him down : Nancy says her father said it was nothing serious."

"Dr. Spalding was wrong," Celia said in a bright hard tone, and shook off Tim's warning hand. "Your father is very ill." She saw the change in Jude's expression with a thrill of pure satisfaction; nothing she had ever said to him before had touched him so near the bone. "He is not going to die, not just now, but that is the kind of illness he has. I know what you are going to say next."

Jude stared at her : she did not find his bewilderment pathetic.

"You are going to say, shall I have to give up my chosen career? Shall I be able to carry on with my lovely life, as if nothing terrible were happening to my father and mother?"

"Celia," Tim said, "stop this."

"Weren't you going to say that?" she flung at the boy, "or have you just enough self control to keep the words back? I am sure that is what you are thinking. And Tim, kindly leave me alone! Somebody has to strip the cotton wool off this boy; between you, you have wrapped him up in a thick soft cocoon; he cannot feel a thing except his own wishes, he cannot hear a thing except his own voice uttering them."

"Have you finished?" Tim said, when it became clear that she had. "You know that Janet and his parents wished him not to know."

"I shall go to Janet now," Celia said, with her head high. "I shall tell her what I have done and offer her my resignation."

He went to the door of the music room with her : the sight of her victim was too much for him.

"I was right," she said in the doorway, "and you know it."

"You were right," he said, "but you and I know why you did it."

He felt immediate compunction at the little moan she made, and turned his back on her; she had no further claim on him.

"Is it true, what she said?"

"Which part of what she said?" Tim asked carefully.

"About my father dying?"

"Janet told us he was a very sick man," Tim said, improving

Celia's moral position a little, "and you will have to pretend you know nothing about it; Celia should not have repeated what was spoken in confidence."

"Why pretend? What good will that do?"

Tim's heart sank. "If you cannot see, I don't know how I can tell you. Don't prove to me that Celia was right, I so much want her to have been wrong."

Jude had sat down before one of the music stands, the one with the viola part on it.

"Because of Tess, you mean, so that she and the younger children won't guess that anything is wrong?"

Tim unclenched his hands and watched his knuckles regain their normal colour.

"I am not much good at hiding things. I will try, if you like."

"Yes, try," Tim said.

"Do you think Daniel would play, if Tess has found him—if he knew about my father? So as not to disappoint everyone, I mean?"

"You were ready enough to disappoint everyone yesterday afternoon," Tim said, "or even this morning."

"It is only a school concert," Jude said with difficulty. "Nobody will expect the standard to be very high."

"Mozart will not turn in his grave when he hears what we are doing to him?"

"It won't be the first time he has turned," Jude said grimly.

"You will have to ask Daniel yourself: I should think you might even have to apologise to him."

"I expect I can do that," Jude said; his tone became less even, the tears came. "I can tell him I am sorry, I wish to God I could tell my father."

"You must not," Tim said at once. "He would know at once that you had heard something. And he will have forgiven you already, there is no need for you to say a word."

"I wish it were this time yesterday," Jude said thickly, "and I had kept my mouth shut when Daniel played the sixths all wrong. But it is not much use wishing."

"It is no use at all," Tim said.

The door opened, Ian came in.

"Sorry I am late, I was looking for Jude. Oh, he is here already."

He looked away in confusion, but Jude got up and wiped his eyes on his sleeve.

"Matthew wants you, Jude, Daniel is in his room. I don't know where Tess is, nobody seems to know. Is there any point in our rehearsing, Tim, if Mr. Pinnegar cannot play?"

"Yes, I think there might be," Tim said. "Bring Daniel back with you, Jude, when Matthew has finished with you both. Ian, you and I might tackle the first trio again, and Tess can join in when she gets here."

Jude left them, they began to play. Soon Tess came in, picked up her viola and joined the others. Tim saw that she was quite calm, quite her ordinary self. "Nobody has told her anything," he thought, "and Jude will not, now he understands." But he was wrong, for words spoken out loud are not all the means of communication available to men and women, and when Harry left Tess and she joined Owen and Helen in the matron's office she knew the truth at once, the bald relentless whole; only the details escaped her. She did not know how many years or months her father might have left, what quantities of devotion and patience his sick self might require from her mother; but while the adults smiled and laughed and reassured each other Tess understood as she had failed earlier to do the different tone in Helen's voice, the altered contours of Owen's face. They told her nothing, in words : she saw that she must appear to know nothing. So she said lightly, "If you can spare me, I must rush. Tim is waiting for me : I don't know what he means to do about the concert, I had better find out." When she had gone Owen and Helen turned to congratulate each other on the marvellous ease with which they had deceived her.

XIII

"WHY DON'T YOU go off and find your people, Nancy? There is almost nothing left to sell, and I will keep an eye on the stall if you like."

"The concert starts in twenty minutes: I can stick it out till then. In three weeks' time I shall be leaving, and my parents will have the pleasure of my company until October. We can manage."

"I thought your father was wonderful when Mr. Pinnegar was taken ill," Florence said warmly, "so calm, so decisive. That other doctor from London with the little boy just stood there and did nothing."

"Well, he works in a hospital," Nancy said. "He is a sort of teacher really, and my father says people like that are not much use in emergencies, when they have no shiny apparatus and students hanging about to admire them. And actually," she said, dealing justly with Harry, "he did take Mr. Pinnegar's pulse, I saw him."

"That does not do anybody any good, having their pulse taken," Florence said with quiet scorn. "Do you want a cup of tea, Kate? There are no strawberries left."

"I don't want strawberries or tea. I might have a lemonade, if there is any."

Florence went into the art room and Kate, who had come into the courtyard still in her pleated white tennis dress, breathed into Nancy's ear, "Has Florence missed me?"

"I daresay she has had no time to. She has been run off her feet. Anne and Susan and one or two of the fourth formers helped when it was really hectic."

"Oh, I am glad! I would not like to think I had left her to cope all alone."

"That was how you left her," Nancy said.

"I have had a dreamy afternoon," Kate said, sliding into a

chair and crossing her legs with a glance of frank appreciation for those handsome members. "I expect this has been the best day of my life."

She waited, Nancy said nothing.

"Aren't you going to ask me why?"

"You will tell me. Why should I bother to ask?"

"Peter kissed me," Kate said, and watched her friend through narrow eyes.

"I thought you were playing tennis, not postman's knock."

"When the game was over we picked up the balls together, and our heads bumped. Is there a bruise on my forehead?"

"No," Nancy said, "only a fringe, and satisfaction writ large."

"It must have been the proximity of my slim young body that overcame his self control."

"Or the proximity of your empty young head."

"Nancy, I shall miss you so much next year, when you are not here to help me through this difficult phase of my girlhood."

"Florence will help you," Nancy said. "She is about ten years older than you are in some ways."

"It is such a pity for her; that rather prim manner frightens the boys."

"Other things might frighten them more, if they had any sense. It is a good thing Peter is leaving too, before you have a chance to seduce him."

"What a foul thing to say! Anyhow that is something boys do to girls, not the other way round. You are showing your ignorance, or your envy."

"Am I?" Nancy said in perfect good humour. "You should look up seduction in a dictionary, Kate, if you can spell the word."

"I shall write to Peter every week."

"Then you will certainly need a dictionary."

"It is not my spelling he loves," Kate said grandly.

"Why not? Your spelling is the most lovable thing about you. Now try to hide your happiness; Florence has found you some lemonade. It would be unkind to repay her by telling her what you have just told me."

"Thank you, Florence dear, how sweet you are. You will make some man or other a wonderful wife some day."

"So will you, Kate, I am sure, as long as he is rich enough for your home to be run by servants."

"If there is one thing I have learned at Cilrheddyn," Kate said with a little air of forgiveness, "it is the importance of personal relationships. I do not mean to rush into marriage. To be tied for life to somebody, and find it was all a mistake!"

"Yes," Nancy said, "he would be sorry."

"Cold, clever women, like you will be, Nancy, are in no great danger. I believe you are incapable of passion."

"Not a bit of it. I have been in love ever since I came here. For seven years I have concealed my feelings; there is nobody to equal him."

"Peter?" Florence suggested.

"Ian? Jude? Nancy," Kate screamed, "not Tim?"

"Why, no, you pair of ninnies, Matthew."

"Will you give me your arm, Daniel? I am very tired; I should have stayed in the garden where your father and step-mother left me. They are probably worrying over me at this moment, if they can spare a few moments from worrying over you."

"I am sorry if I have caused a lot of trouble," Daniel said, and let his grandmother place her hand on his warm brown forearm where it felt as dry and light as a bird's foot.

"Yes, it is all very well to say that, that is what all young people say when it is too late and the damage is done. Dinah is young, of course, and takes everything easily, that is her great charm; and your father is too much a man of the world to allow us to guess everything he feels. But you might have spared a little thought, Dan, for the pain you were causing me."

"I did think of you," Daniel said with a red face. "I thought of all of you, but it made no difference."

Mrs. Daintry stopped in her tracks half way up the dusty track with honeysuckle and blue sky overhead, and the voices of Harry and his child, Tess and her little sister fading as they turned the corner.

"You can speak to me, dear, you can tell me anything there is to tell quite freely. You know that I can keep a secret, we have had so many little secrets together in the past."

Daniel looked down at her, and at her fingers fastened on his wrist: she was not to be shaken off, she was not to be silenced.

"I understand it all now, dear; that boy is jealous of you, he knows his sister is throwing herself at your head, and so he does his best to make you miserable."

Certainly Daniel looked miserable enough: she took from his silence strength to continue.

"I shall have a word with your father: there is surely something that can be done. And the boy is leaving at the end of the term, so there is no need for you to stand this persecution any longer. As for the girl, no doubt a word from Miss Storace will be enough, and she will leave you alone."

Restraint snapped in the boy like an overwound watch spring; his arm jerked up, and Muriel teetered on her tiny feet. Her hand, rejected, came up to her mouth.

"Daniel!"

He swallowed the words that rose to his lips and walked on ahead of her with his head down; but after a few steps an older habit reasserted itself, he stopped and waited for her.

"I am sorry, Gran."

"Yes, I should think you would be. What sort of manners do they teach you in this terrible place, what does your father pay out half his income for, if you are to grow up as much of a lout as that other boy?"

"Jude is not a lout," Daniel said patiently enough, "and the fees are not nearly half Dad's income, and Cilrheddyn is only terrible to you because it is not like any school you would have chosen for a child of your own. So you ought to be the first one to hear the good news, Gran; Dad will be paying no more fees, and you will never have to set foot in this place again. I am going to ask them to take me away."

She searched his face doubtfully: such total capitulation to her hopes and wishes expressed with such freedom, without any overt prompting on her part, frightened her into a rapid disavowal.

"Whatever are you saying, dear? What will your father think, and Dinah, after all they have sacrificed for you, all they have counted on?"

"I never asked for any sacrifice. I don't know what they may have been counting on. I can't stay here any longer."

He walked on as he spoke; his grandmother, her fatigue forgotten in the terrified delight he aroused in her, almost ran after him for the last few yards uphill to the school gates. At those gates he stopped, and she caught him up, a little short of breath, but rosy with exhilaration.

"You are not to say anything to my parents," he said, and never observed how she flinched away from the term that brought Vincent and Dinah closer than she cared. "I shall tell them as much as I can as soon as I see them."

"Yes, Daniel, if you say so. I promised," she said, in an attempt to regain her lost advantage, "I would keep any little secret you asked me to; I told you you could speak to me freely."

But her loss was permanent, he would not minimise it.

"There is no secret, there is only what I said, I am going to leave Cilrheddyn. But I prefer to tell Dad myself, and Dinah will have to hear it at the same time."

"I wonder where they will have got to?" Muriel said, looking about the courtyard.

"If you will sit in the shade, Gran, I will go and find them."

"I will come with you, dear. I am just a little tired of being left on chairs as if I were a parcel people were sick of carrying."

Daniel clenched his fists inside his pockets, but succour was at hand, in Ian's shambling form.

"Dan, Matthew wants you in his study : as soon as you got back, he said; he said to tell you that he has seen your parents and they know you are safe, and want you to go to him before they see you."

Muriel sank down on to a chair with a tight little smile of resignation.

"Go then, dear, if Mr. Storace considers that he has the first claim. Your family can wait."

"Have you a grandmother?" Daniel said to Ian as they went off together.

"One is dead, and the other is in Australia."

"And they say all men are created equal," Daniel said, with a long low laugh, quite devoid of mirth.

"Here he is, Emma, none the worse for a little time away from us, as you can see."

But Emma's eyes saw further than Harry's : she could not miss the pallor of her son's face, his dragging steps as he followed

Harry into the library where all the plates were empty of sandwiches and hardly a cake was left.

"Are you hungry, dear? Harry, there seems to be plenty of tea, perhaps Robert could have some with lots of sugar."

"I don't want any."

"Nonsense, you will have what your mother thinks right for you."

Robert's face puckered; Meg came forward swiftly with a glass of orange juice and an iced bun on a plate.

"Will you have these, if Mummy says you may? Clare likes fruit drinks better than tea," she said to Emma, "and glasses are easier to hold than cups if they are not sitting at a table."

Robert took what she offered, and did not look at Harry or Emma, who said with an attempt at cheerfulness that did nothing to conceal her strange heaviness of heart, "There, Harry! Miss Lindsay understands little boys better than we do."

"I should," Meg said, "I spend most of my time with them. Did my daughter come back with you, Professor Branksome?"

"Yes, and some other children, that boy Diggory and his sisters, and the older boy who seemed to be lost earlier on. He has gone to Mr. Storace, I believe. I don't know where the others went, the big girl is with her father. How is he, do you know?"

"Better than they had imagined; he took some tablets, and sat in a darkened room. It is a wretched thing to happen, today of all days; the concert will probably be cancelled. We should know quite soon; Mr. Pinnegar was to play with the children, and that is out of the question now."

Emma's disappointment would not be concealed.

"Did you mean to stay, after all?" Meg said. "I will take care of Robert, if you like, if there is anything to stay for. I promise I won't leave him to Clare's tender mercies again."

"No, it is very kind of you, Miss Lindsay, but it is too much, you have had quite enough of our son for one day. You will want to hear the music yourself."

"I don't care for music," Meg said. "I shall be far happier outside than shut up in the music room for an hour. I am sacrificing nothing, honestly."

"I am not musical, either," Harry said, "and Emma is right, we have no business to keep taking advantage of you. I will look after Robert, and Emma can enjoy herself without feeling that she is spoiling your afternoon."

Meg might have said something more, Emma almost thought she heard the intake of breath that comes before a quick rejoinder; but if she did, no words followed, only a slight shrug of the shoulders, as if for resignation. The younger woman moved away to speak to Celia, and then crossed the library to join another group of parents. The Branksomes were left with each other, not quite at ease, neither quite daring to understand the reason for their discomfiture.

"Well, Robert!" Harry said, when a strange minute or two had passed and nothing had been said to dispel the strangeness, "what do you think of Cilrheddyn? How do you like the place?"

"Oh, Harry, not here, not now! Wait until we are alone with him."

"Supposing he tells us it is all horrible : he has done that once already, told me at least, not half an hour ago. I hope you won't imagine I have influenced his views."

"Please, Harry!" his wife said, with a look almost of supplication.

"Nobody is listening, nobody is taking any notice of us."

"Robert is listening."

"Robert, if you have finished your tea, you may go outside. I will join you in a moment."

"I don't want to go : I want to stay with Mummy."

"When Mummy goes to the music room for the concert you and I will go for a walk."

"I will stay with Mummy," Robert said, with a throb in his voice that all three of them knew to be a danger signal.

"We will see, dear," Emma said. "Perhaps there won't be a concert at all. It would be silly to get into a state about something that may not happen."

"It is not the concert that he is getting into a state about. It is the prospect of an hour alone with me."

"He slept so little last night, and today must have been a great strain for him, so many new faces and places, a day unlike any he has ever spent before."

"It is clear enough he will not want to spend one like it again."

Emma said swiftly and clearly, drawing upon some depth of perception outside her daily range, "Whatever it is that has upset you and made you angry, Harry, it is not Robert, and it is not the school. You do nothing justice, yourself least of all, when you are so wilfully blind to the facts of the situation."

"What facts?" he now demanded. "What situation?"

"Robert," Emma said, "Miss Lindsay is going out of the room. Run after her and ask her if you may go swimming. Would you like that?"

"Yes. But how can I? I have no swimming trunks."

"I am sure she will borrow some for you."

The child caught an unaccustomed note in his mother's voice, and did as he was told. As soon as he had gone she said, "Now you are to go after them both. If there is no concert I shall find somewhere quiet to sit : you need not hurry for my sake."

"Emma, what is it? What do you want me to do? I am absolutely at a loss, I cannot understand you."

"It is yourself you cannot understand," she said. "Miss Lindsay will help you : ask her, and see. I am going to talk to the Hardys; they will have news of their son."

She suited her action to the words, leaving him to join Vincent and Dinah who stood selfconsciously in an embrasure as if they hoped or feared to be asked for autographs. He watched her go; then did as she had told him, responding to the same steely quality in her voice that had sent Robert from them almost at a run.

"When my sister and I bought this house," Matthew said, "that story was one of the first things we knew about it. The estate agent seemed to think it was a selling point, at the same level as the swimming pool or the rose garden. I used to catch myself looking at the chimney breasts in the different rooms and wondering, which one?"

Daniel's eyes went to the fireplace; it gave away no secrets.

"There was no way of telling. For a time it was almost an obsession : I wanted to know if the child was burned to death, or suffocated by a fall of soot, or if the flues were so intricate that he was actually lost up there and starved in the darkness. That was an absurd idea, for he would have cried out, and somebody would have broken down a wall and got him out."

"Would they?" Daniel said.

"Yes, I think so. They were not knowingly doing evil, sending a child of eight up a chimney, after all. It was only what anyone might have done at that time, if the child had his living to make, and there were no factories or mines near enough for him to work in, and no need of him on any of the farms round about. They never planned to cripple or kill him, very few men ever plan to do such things : but indolence and lack of imagination will do as much harm as wickedness, and they are commoner and more easily excused."

Daniel's look said plainly that he could find no excuses.

"Janet told me you put flowers on his grave. When did you know about him?"

"In the spring term. I went down one evening, there must have been a service the Sunday before, the graveyard was all tidied up. I began to read the names on the headstones." After a long silence he said, "My mother has no headstone, no grave, really. She didn't want one, she asked for her ashes to be scattered in a place where she and my father used to stay. Everyone thinks that is a good idea when father tells them, Dinah says she would feel just the same."

Matthew waited, a thing he was used to doing.

"I started to look for children's graves, there are quite a lot of them at one end of the churchyard, I suppose there was an epidemic or something. Then I saw this one, away from the others. I never thought about chimney sweeps before, I always hated that book about the water babies. And of course it is all over, there is no point in being angry about it now."

"You found other things to make you angry. There is never any shortage, after all."

"I did those translations," Daniel said leaving Matthew momentarily far behind. "A year ago I used to repeat some of the Rimbaud poems over to myself by the hour, I suppose I drugged myself with them; the sound of the words was enough, I didn't bother with the meaning. I thought it would be splendid to be a writer, just working on a few lines until they were so beautiful they made other people feel like that, drunk, but not horrible the way drunks are; and I did write some poems. One of them was about not having a mother, I thought I might have been rather lucky; Florence lent me *Sons and Lovers*, and you can see how bloody it must have been for him, being torn in pieces by those women. And then I felt as if I had wished my mother dead. That was why I went to the graveyard, I suppose. I don't remember any other reason, just feeling that the dead get the worst of everything, and there was no way of telling her I was sorry."

"Have you ever talked to your step-mother about this?"

"Dinah is so clever, it is no use talking to her. You tell her something you have just thought of and she sees into it and all round it, and she can tell you why you thought of it, and why it means so much to you, and if you say it doesn't mean much at all she smiles and nods, but you know she doesn't believe you." He added, with some compunction, "I like Dinah, I wouldn't like you to think I don't know how lucky I am, having her for a step-mother."

Matthew did not comment on his luck, or on Dinah. Instead, he said reluctantly, "You organised the exhibition in the outhouse. You wrote the captions and cut out the photographs; and it was because of the chimney sweep and your mother, and your sense of the injustice of their deaths, and other wastes of other lives." And when Daniel's face confirmed this, though he said nothing, Matthew went on, "I would like to have known sooner : I have watched you change in the last six months. We thought you were perhaps outgrowing us, needing new people and places. Janet and I have seen that happen, and it is painful, it is a thing we never get used to, but we know how necessary it is. I won't tell you to be patient, to wait until you know what you want, as I have told some others, because I don't think another year or two would make any difference. You are not going to forget what you have learned; you have found out the difference between your own life and the hideous lives that have to be lived somehow."

Daniel said, "I wish I could say I wanted to be a missionary or a doctor or something, I wish I could want to do something useful. Then I could stay here and go on to university and feel there was some sense in it. Perhaps later on I shall feel like that, just now all I want is to be on my own as much as I can." After a pause he said, "The worst things that happen here are only pinpricks really, and even quite bad things are understood, most of the time, anyway."

"Then perhaps I ought not to say that I understand, since that is what you would almost rather I didn't. Will your father understand, do you think?"

A change in the quality of the boy's attentiveness made Matthew look up with his last words, and some more pieces of the puzzle fell into place.

"Then it is partly because of your father that you have to go."

Daniel had stifled his shame and exasperation long enough; the boy now said much that he would regret later, and Matthew let him go on and on, offering no comment, trusting that regret would lead in time to some pity for Vincent and knowing very well that it would then be his turn to play the villain in Daniel's story.

"Either he writes lies, week after week, and makes money out of them, and uses that money quite coldly and cynically to send me here, or he writes what he thinks is true and is afraid to test it, in case it turns out to be false."

"You are his only child," Matthew said at last. "Perhaps that is something you should take into account. He would not want you to suffer to prove a theory for him, and you had been wretched at two state schools before you came here."

"Then what right has he to tell everybody such schools are wonderful? Jude's father teaches in one, and sends his children here."

"Then he must be a hypocrite too, perhaps we are all hypocrites by your standards. Janet and I are not sure that education should be bought and sold, and yet we run this place. That puts us on a level with anybody's parents, or even lower."

"What happens to people?" Daniel said, as if this was something Matthew could tell him.

"Many of them have children," Matthew said. "Janet and I have not even that excuse. Your father has; or rather he has you, one child, not to be used as an experimental animal. A few people would do that even with their own one child."

Daniel raised his head and met Matthew's mild look that seemed to offer no resistance.

"You are trying to make me see my father's point of view."

"I am suggesting that he has one. You made him sound as if he only existed by virtue of your indignation."

A silence followed; Daniel returned to the study of his hands, folded in his lap with an appearance of docility. Jude knocked on the door and came in at the sound of Matthew's voice.

"Yes, I am expecting you : I have two things to say to you, Jude, and one involves Daniel so we will deal with that first."

Daniel got out of his chair with a look of alarm.

"If it is about what happened yesterday at the rehearsal, it was my fault : I played abominably, I was thinking of something else. I deserved all he said. My going off like that was nothing to do with Jude."

"I should not have said what I did," Jude said with his eyes on Matthew, "but I expect I would say it again if I had to; I promised Tim I would apologise so that you would play at the concert : I can't do it properly because I am not properly sorry."

"Does Tim want me to play?"

"Yes, and Tess and Ian would like it. And I am only one out of five, so the majority ought to prevail. And actually I would sooner we got through it somehow rather than waste all that work, and my father would like to hear it, if his headache is gone. I wish I could just say I was sorry, I know it would sound better."

"No, it would not," Daniel said. "I should know it was a lie, anyway. I will play, if you will promise to keep on to the very end, however awful it is. If it is awful you can tell me afterwards when everybody has gone. I don't mind that."

Matthew looked at his watch.

"You have ten minutes, Daniel : find Tim and tell him Jude will be ready in time. And if you want to tell your father what you have just told me, do it now, and say that I will write to him tomorrow. You must not hurt him any longer by your secrecy; he deserves something better."

Daniel left them; Matthew motioned to Jude to sit down, but Jude remained standing.

"I know what it is. Meg told me she would have to report me to you, for leaving the third formers alone after I had been told to sleep in their dormitory."

"What is to be done about it, Jude?"

"I will sleep with them for the rest of the term. Daniel can have my tent."

"He prefers to sleep inside : you cannot choose to punish yourself by making someone else uncomfortable."

"I cannot think of anything else," Jude said at last. "Whatever I did wouldn't alter what happened last night."

"Would you do the same thing again, in the same circumstances?"

"No," Jude said without hesitation.

"But you would say bitter and hurtful words to Daniel again, if you had yesterday back?"

"Yes," Jude said, "because I was right; I have thought about it, and I know I was right."

"And were you right to say the same things to your father this morning?"

"It is not my fault he is ill," Jude said, "and if he were not ill he would have known I was right too. I can't help it, that is how I see it."

"Go away and get ready to play then," Matthew said, with a slight movement of weariness. "I shall be listening with a very critical ear : if you are going to trade in your humanity for your gifts, they will need to be very great gifts, or we shall all lose by it."

When his door had closed behind the second boy his thoughts returned to the first and to other boys before him, and to some girls too; for those moments in their lives Jude and Daniel thought unique and extraordinary had been lived before, had required to be lived by many others : and a succession of such moments observed or suffered by Matthew had made him what he was as surely as they had formed the younger lives he now reviewed, feeling himself solitary, passive, old, of little use.

"There, that is better," Meg said, taking a step back from Tamsin to survey the results of a few minutes' work with needle and thread. "I will do your hair for you and then you will look fresh and neat in time for the concert."

She undid the child's plaits with deft fingers and brushed them out; then made a long parting from crown to nape and tied each side with a bow of ribbon.

"That is not how Mummy does it."

"No, but it is easier this way, and I have not had as much practice as your mother."

"Thank you, Meg."

"Are you going with Tamsin, Clare?"

"No. Who wants to sit in a stuffy old music room? I am going swimming."

"Get your things, then. There is a dry towel behind the door."

"Here is that boy," Clare said. "Why is he always coming bothering us?"

"Be quiet, Clare. He is only here for the day, after all."

Robert came into Meg's room without knocking, averting his eyes from Clare's naked body.

"My mother says I am to go swimming, if you can find anything for me to wear."

"Put your bathing suit on, Clare. I think I could lay my hands on something, Robert. Wait here."

Clare wriggled and stretched; once decently covered she began to dance round Robert.

"Why don't you swim bare?"

"I don't like to."

"I do often, in the holidays when there is nobody around."

"It is not holidays now. Your mother wouldn't like it."

"How do you know what my mother would like?"

"I don't suppose she is different from other mothers."

"She is prettier," Clare said. "She is prettier and younger than Diggory's or yours."

Harry's shadow fell through the doorway of Meg's room; the children fell silent.

"Where is Miss Lindsay?" he said to the child, conscious of an awkwardness.

"She is looking for bathing trunks for me," Robert said, and as Meg came in and handed him a pair with her eyes on Harry, "Who is Sam Trousdell?" he asked, inspecting the name tape.

"He is a third former," Meg said. "He is a lot older than you but not very much bigger, and these are made of stretchy stuff so I expect they will do. Clare, come outside with me while Robert changes."

"Why? It is our room, not his."

"He is our guest," Meg said in a repressive voice. "Do you want me?" she said to Harry. "Were you looking for me, I mean?"

"I was following my son," Harry said, explaining nothing.

"Yes, of course."

Robert came out of Meg's room.

"You are very white," Clare said, "only bits of your arms and legs are a nice colour. I am brown nearly all over."

"London is a poor place to get a sun tan," Meg said. "Bring another towel for Robert, Clare."

"He can bring it himself," Clare said, and threw him one.

XIV

Somebody, perhaps Janet, had had the foresight to draw the curtains of the music room during the early afternoon; though Tim had parted them for his rehearsal at four the worst of the heat had been shut out, and now the sun had moved off that side of the building and the air in the long white room though warm was not intolerable. Nevertheless Tim sweated, and wiped his palms on his handkerchief as parents and children filed in, obstinately refusing to sit in the front seats; out of shyness, he supposed, though the audience was not there to be looked at, after all. When Kate came in she took a prominent seat and crossed her legs with deliberate grace; this broke the spell. Peter and his parents joined her, Nancy and her father, the Pinnegars not without sideways glances of uncertainty, began to fill the row. Ian was already in his place, now Tess joined him; a moment later Daniel in a clean shirt and long trousers came in and went to his music stand. The hum of voices seemed to some ears as sensitive as Tim's to drop appreciably with the boy's appearance, to rise again, to swell, finally to mingle with a little outburst of clapping when Janet and Matthew took their places.

"Where is Jude?" Tim said to Tess under his breath.

"He will be here; he had to wash."

"You are sure he is not going to let us down at the last moment?"

Her look silenced him; a minute later Jude joined them, and Tess smiled at Tim, and across the room to her father.

"Your face is almost as red as my dress," she said to her brother. "What have you been doing, scrubbing it?"

"No, I am blushing, in case anyone thought I made a delayed entrance on purpose."

"Did you?"

"No, Matthew kept me. Hadn't you better tune up?"

He played a single pellucid note, the others approached it with varying degrees of success; a hush fell upon the audience, such is the magical effect of four stringed instruments uttering disconnected sounds. Soon the sounds coalesced and became tolerable. Tim stood up.

"Janet and Matthew, parents, children, I put some programmes on your chairs, but really there is no need of them, because we are only going to play one work. Usually we have songs and solos and recitations; but this year we thought we would do something different because this is Jude Pinnegar's last year with us, and a time will come when we shall all of us have to pay to hear him, and when some of you who are with us today will be glad and proud to have been present on a mildly historical occasion."

There was applause, some of it a trifle sardonic in character; Jude studied his music as if it were new to him, Tess tingled with delight on his behalf, embarrassment on her own.

"It is no use pretending the rest of us are up to his standard; but if he can put up with our deficiencies, I am sure all of you in your generosity can do as much. Here it is, then, Mozart's Clarinet Quintet in A major, K. 581, in four movements, *allegro*, *larghetto, minuetto* with two trios, and an *allegretto* with variations, and I may as well warn you now that some of them are very difficult."

He sat down, mopping his brow. Daniel tucked his violin under his chin and wondered if he would be able to keep time when his heart was thumping so loudly; but Tim's eyes, and Ian's, Tess's and even Jude's, were upon him. He tapped his foot, his young hoarse voice rang out, "One, two, three, four," and in orderly quietness the first subject was stated by all the strings and given poignancy by the clarinet a moment later, soaring above them, bearing them up from plangent depths; each note was rounded and radiant, the succession like drops of water at the edge of a fountain, each rendered bright and hard as a diamond by the light of summer.

"I ought to apologise for my daughter," Meg said, as they followed the children down the stairs and out of a side door into the garden.

"Why should you? Nobody expects politeness from a child of

that age. If she doesn't like Robert there is no reason why she should pretend to. There will be time enough for pretence when she is older."

Sunshine flashed off the swimming pool, its surface was hardly ruffled, and Clare slipped into it with no more disturbance than a fish might have made. Robert stood on the brink, uncertain whether or not to jump.

"He has had swimming lessons," Harry said, and raised his voice. "In you go now, Robert. Don't let a girl show you up."

Robert sat on the edge and dipped a toe in.

"It is awfully cold."

"Only for the first few moments. And that is half the point of swimming on a hot day, to get cool."

Since there was no help for it, the boy lowered himself in. Clare swam close to him, stood up, shook a shower of glittering drops over him and laughed at his outraged scarlet face.

"Clare!" Meg shouted, but Harry laid his hand upon her arm.

"Leave them, she will do him no harm, he takes everything too hard."

Robert began to splash, to leap, to shout, to flail water over Clare in glancing webs of iridescence; she went beneath the surface, he followed and came up spluttering and retching.

"You are all right," Harry called. "Don't let a girl get the better of you!"

"Why not?" Meg said, "if she can do it?"

His hand was on her arm still; he had been quite unaware of this until the cold anger of her voice struck him and he instantly took it away.

"What world is this you live in?" she said, with a hard edge on the words, "where everything is to be a struggle, and somebody has to win or lose?"

"It is the world you live in," he said in a subdued way, keeping his eyes on the children in the glassy water. "I should have thought you would have recognised it, after all that has happened to you."

"Nothing has happened to me that I can recognise as a loss," Meg said.

Harry laughed; she thought she had never heard a laugh with less mirth in it, or more incredulity.

"You are only twenty years older than your daughter: you

were hardly more than a child yourself when you conceived her. Well, you have at least learnt to pretend : are you doing it for my sake, or for your own?"

"If I were pretending," she said carefully, "it would not be for my sake. There is no reason that I know of why I should do it for yours."

"Then it is for your child's sake. How long do you believe that you can keep it up?"

"It is no pretence that I enjoy the life that I have chosen, I find real satisfaction in it."

"Do you expect me to believe that, that a girl as intelligent as you are could be content with this existence?"

"You know very little about this existence, as you call it."

"I have been watching you all day, wondering how you could stand it, being at the beck and call of teachers and parents, of boys and girls no more talented than you are, most of them probably not half so clever."

"What do you know about my cleverness?" she said, turning upon him a look of pure wonderment. "I was only one term in the medical school, I sat for no examinations there, I was never even on one of your ward rounds; whatever reputation I made for myself was not related to my intelligence."

"When you had left," he said, after a pause that threatened to become painful, "I looked into your records, I spoke to some of the clinical teachers about you; it was clear that you were an outstanding student."

"Thank you. For looking into my records, I mean. I am surprised that you could spare time to do anything so pointless."

"I would have liked to help you in some way : I am not saying this because I want any gratitude. Nothing came of it, it was just an impulse. Now I wish I had pursued it further."

"Oh, I am glad you didn't!" she cried.

"So this is what it feels like," Nancy said to herself, "to be on the threshold of the future, or whatever they call it. To be leaving school, anyway, to be going out into the world. I suppose a university is the world, or more of it than school could be. And later there will be medical school, and working in hospitals, perhaps in laboratories; many more men than women so that there ought to be a chance of marriage even for me, as Kate would kindly put it. And what will Kate do without me if she wears dresses as short as that, with such fine stockings, too? She will have to look for someone else to dream and scheme about next year with Peter gone, and Jude and Ian. Who will it be? The younger boys are so much younger, perhaps she will turn her attention to the staff: but most of them are married, not that that would deter her. Supposing she tried to start something with the Spaniards, they are handsome enough: I have seen them looking at her in the evenings when she stands outside her tent lifting her hair to tie it in a pony tail. Oh, Kate, not the Spaniards, please! Though I do not know why I should care, she is nothing to me, in a few years' time I shall hardly remember her, her lovely face, her silly talk."

"I am glad Peter does not play anything," Kate said. "If they knew how silly they look, Jude is as red as a turkeycock after every long passage, Tim sweats like a pig, Ian straddles his 'cello as if he were planning to ride it round the room, and what a nice change that would make. Daniel looks all right, to be fair; that lock of hair falling over his brow is quite romantic. Next year he will be in the sixth form and so shall I; with Peter gone I might consider helping Daniel to overcome his shyness. Tess says he is leaving, she may be leaving herself, but how would Tess know? There is her mother, I hope Tess takes warning by her: why do nice women look so awful, their hair, their flowery dresses, their shoes, their hair! At least I need not feel the least bit ashamed of my mother, her lipstick is perfect, I hope she will let me borrow it. I rather wish Daddy could have come, though he would have hated this. Tootling and scraping, he calls it, this kind of music, and of course he would not want to be here when Mummy is, it makes things awkward for both of them."

"The examinations are over," Peter said. "Now Ian and I can get down to making those scale drawings: in three weeks we should be able to produce a working model. I hope Kate will not expect me to dance attendance on her till the end of term. I shall play tennis with her sometimes, I shall need the exercise and fresh air. I daresay she will want me to dance with her at the end of term hop; perhaps Nancy will keep her out of the way."

"If Kate were leaving and Peter were staying," Florence said, "I should have a year of purest heaven to look forward to instead of deepest, blackest hell. There is a poem in that somewhere, things always happening to the wrong people at the wrong time. I wonder if anybody would notice if I wrote on the back of my programme, resting it on my knee? No, they would think I was making notes on the music. Bother Mozart, this rhythm is so insistent that I can't write against it; I shall have to wait. How awful life is, the artist's life anyway, especially if the artist is a nice young girl. Rimbaud would simply get up and walk out and write his poem and not care a damn about what anybody thought. I can't really be going to be a poet or I would be able to do that, just say to them, 'I am very sorry, but I have something to do, will you excuse me?' But of course they would not excuse me, they would just think I didn't know how to behave."

"You understand that I knew nothing of your pregnancy; my wife only told me yesterday when we were on our way here."

"I asked her to keep it a secret," Meg said, but did not say how surprised she was that Emma had kept it so well.

"Yes, she said she had made you a promise, Emma does not make promises lightly. All the same, I wish I had known."

"Why? What could you have done about it?"

"I would have seen to it that you faced the facts of the matter; that you realised to the full what having a child would mean to you, in your position."

"Your wife did that, or tried to. But she is kind and imaginative, so she did not do it very well. And in any case I was not such a fool as you seem to have thought. I knew what I was doing; nobody forced me to have my child and keep her."

That child came out of the pool and sat beside them, kicking up the water with her brown feet, the skin of her insteps ridged and gleaming. "What you have given up for her!" Harry breathed.

"London, one sort of life, a succession of lovers, perhaps, and perhaps a succession of abortions."

"You know what I mean," he said.

"I think perhaps I am beginning to," she said, turning away from him in sudden dread of her own power.

"Well," Tim said to himself, "the allegro could have been much worse. Daniel is playing remarkably well, I hope it is not because he is afraid of what Jude may say to him afterwards. It is too soon to feel complacent, though, there are much worse things to come. Tess is abstracted, some of her turns have not been all they should be, but I cannot tell her now; unless I were just to press the side of her foot. Would she know that that was what I meant? She is not Kate, so it is worth trying."

"That was a strange look I saw Tess give Tim," Celia said, "almost as if he had startled her in some way : now she is smiling. I don't know what she has to smile about, but perhaps she is just thankful that Jude is making such a splendid impression. How heartless they are at that age, how resilient! I thought I had put it out of his power to make any sort of show in public this afternoon, but he does not suffer, I do it for him. God knows why I dragged myself here, I would rather be lying on my bed with the curtains drawn. I wish I had taken two aspirins, one is not nearly enough for such a headache."

"Now here is the lovely long-drawn out bit," Janet said, "that I would like to hear over and over again, if that were not to risk making it seem too ordinary; and if it were properly played, of course, though Daniel is doing very well. What a pity Tim had to choose something so difficult! Next year he will go back to more ordinary pieces; that will be dull, but safer. Sometimes people like Jude are almost more trouble than they are worth. But I shall miss him, and Daniel too. Five years is a long time; they come looking and behaving like Diggory, and before I can see any great difference in my face or Matthew's their faces have changed almost out of recognition. Now the lovely bit again, but less of it, so that one is always left wishing for more. And the triplets descend, and Daniel does his best, I hope his father is proud of him, even though the triplets are not quite even. Nobody can do everything, after all."

"Trying to be mother and father to a child is too much for anyone," Harry said. "If Charles had known you were to have a baby he might have made provision for you. I would have seen to it that he made provision."

"At your sister's expense," Meg said, "and her little girls'? I find it strange to think of Clare having half-sisters; I don't expect you to believe me, but I can hardly realise now that she has a father. How is Charles?"

"He is all right. He is doing very well, financially, I mean. Women patients are drawn to him."

"And their husbands pay the bills. What a lucky man he is," Meg said without bitterness, but Harry could not hear such a statement, at least from her, with equal charity.

"I tried to make him feel what he had done, spoiling your future, changing the whole course of your life, though neither of us knew how much. I would have made a scandal of it, but you put a stop to that; your leaving the medical school of your own free will made it impossible for me to get justice for you by exposing him."

"Did you never think you might get justice for him by exposing me? I remember I told you at the time I was not innocent; Charles did nothing with me or to me that I did not ask for, and I knew that he was married. I did not like myself when it was all over."

"And do you now? Do you like the woman you have become?"

He thought she did not hear him, her head was turned away, she waved briefly to her daughter and his son.

"I am the same woman, ten years older, or nearly. I have learned what I am capable of, for good or ill."

"It seems to me that you are using your child as a scourge," he said.

"Children are used," she said. "You could hardly work among them for many years without finding that out."

"To prove some idiotic theory or other!" he said in scorn, yet showed that this pleased him too, confirming his worst suspicions. She looked at him for a long time, allowing his tone to linger in her mind and spell out for her clearly the danger she might put herself in, were she not aware of it.

"I did not say the school used them," she said finally.

"Daniel is playing beautifully," Mrs. Daintry said right out loud in the gap between the second and third movements, so that people either turned to look at her or carefully avoided doing this, according to their natures. "I do not know," she said to Dinah at her side, "why that other boy should be given all the credit, I am sure I have read somewhere that the violin is harder to play than the clarinet." She subsided, at least to outward appearances, as the minuet began. "It is not just because he is leaving, either, our boy is leaving, too; some acknowledgement should be made of that fact, and of his courage in playing at all in the circumstances. To sleep a whole night in that empty church! What does that say for this splendid school, when a boy prefers a hard bench and the company of mice to anything the Storaces can provide for him? It is all nonsense about his going to a state school, and it is far too late for any public school to take him, even the very minor ones, and in some ways that would be almost worse; it is awful to mention the name of a place and then have to explain it. But there are those places in the West End, no fuss over Common Entrance, or perhaps something might be arranged with a private tutor. And at any rate he will be at home. He will be there when I get up in the morning and I shall be there when he comes home in the afternoon. Dinah need not fear that he will be kept waiting for his meals, and she and Vincent will not need to stay at home in the evenings, or curtail their holidays for his sake."

"Muriel at least will be happy," Dinah told herself, "she is happy now, tapping her foot in three time. Later she will tell me how pretty the minuet was, how she loves these old dances with their dignity and charm. She will imply that they danced nothing but minuets and sarabandes when she was a girl, and if I mention the Charleston or the tango she will sulk for several days. And yet at other times if I suggest she might like an early night or breakfast in bed she flares up at once, and accuses me of making her out to be senile. I shall be like that myself one day, I suppose, and since I have no children of my own, not even one to mourn for when everyone is busy or away, perhaps I shall be even worse. And Daniel is fond of her, though she gets on his nerves. They often say there is especial sympathy between the old and the very young; we did work in a thing about that, in one of the earliest episodes, the old school caretaker who was crusty and disagreeable but understood that curious child so much better than anyone else. Would he have understood Dan, I wonder, does Muriel have any idea what is going on in his mind? I certainly don't, I have all sorts of explanations ready, so many that none of them can be right. He talked to Vincent in my presence, and I felt as if I were not there, I would have liked to go away, there was nothing I could do for either of them. Now I know what that silly cliché means, words fail me, for they really did. I feel ashamed of myself, my being left out hardly matters after all. I don't think Vincent could have foreseen this, and whatever Muriel says now it came as a shock to her. I saw how she looked when they came back together from the church; she is no nearer to him than we are, he does not want any of us. For Vincent's sake I smiled and smiled and hinted that we should all have a splendid time together, but I know in my heart that the next year or two will be hell, it is a time that will have to be got through somehow, and my job will be to keep the three of them from destroying each other right under my eyes."

"This, then, was the form it had to take," Vincent said, "and having read one's Freud helps very little, which seems unfair when people who have never set eyes on one of his books seem to derive so much benefit from using his terms with no regard for their meaning. My son despises me; he thinks I am shallow, a timeserver, a hypocrite. He would like me better if I were a failure, for then he could defend me against his own contempt. He is generous enough for that, his generosity is the keenest weapon he possesses. I wish I could think like Dinah; I wish I could believe that he wants to come home in order to be with her : or like Mother, that it is because Cilrheddyn was not good enough for him, nobody understands him here, or puts the right value upon him. But I may be shallow without being false, and Matthew recognises that and knows that I can meet truth with truth. It is only because Cilrheddyn has been the best place for him for five years or more that it is the wrong place now; and for that we shall have to be thankful, now or later."

"Five more minutes, Clare. I saw you shivering."

Clare went under again, to hide her gooseflesh. Robert climbed out of the pool, shaking drops from him like a dog.

"Mind what you are doing!" Harry said. "Look, you have made Miss Lindsay's dress wet."

"Never mind, it will dry in a few minutes. Here is your towel, Robert. Now, Clare, out you come."

"Why should I?" Clare called and shot across the pool away from them.

"Because your mother says so," Harry called after her in a

roar that was no less absurd for being totally ineffective. To her disregarded mother he said in a baffled way, "I do not see how you can stand it, the disobedience, the tempers, the silly inane talk all day long."

"Yes, it is awful. But other people's children are easier to manage than one's own, and there is enough special feeling left to make the difference. Most of the time I can be patient with her. Her childhood will not last for ever."

"In about five minutes it will be over," Diggory said to Tamsin in a loud whisper. "Surely you can wait that long?" He turned away from her as if her quiet misery offended him. "It is always the same," his memory informed him. "The very first Parents' Day of all when Tess was younger than I am now and Jude was still at home she was sick during the concert or perhaps it was a play or people saying poems. I remember her being sick, but I have forgotten what everyone else was doing. They say as you grow older you only remember the nice things, but I think they lie. I am almost sure they lie."

"I hate Diggory," Tamsin said in reddened silence, willing the tears not to flow. "I rushed back from his silly churchyard and Meg sent me to wash and mended my dress, there was no time to go to the lavatory and anyhow I didn't want to then. I will sit with my legs crossed like Kate and press my thighs together hard and think about something different. This has been the worst day of my life, and I am glad, glad, glad, that I shall never come to Cilrheddyn, I would like never to come here again even to see Tess and Diggory. Tess and I are nice, and Jude is not so bad, why should we have a brother like Diggory? This music goes on for ever and that bit sounded queer : Daddy looked at Mummy and they both looked at Jude, but it was the violin that went wrong, and it is going wrong again. The first time I came here I was sick all over my lap, I wish I did not have to remember that now, Diggory is remembering too. We might almost be twins, if I were not so much nicer than he is. My dress smelt awful, Meg took me away and washed it and found an old one of somebody else's to go home in. Meg is kind, though she does not say much."

"What more is there to say?" Meg said equably. "In ten or

twelve years' time she will be grown up, and I shall look about for another sort of job."

"Ten or twelve years! Life imprisonment lasts very little longer."

"Yes, but the conditions are different. Warders are not friends, and I turn the key in my own lock, I can vary the length of my own sentence."

"You will not find it so easy to get interesting work when you are over forty," he said with conscious brutality. "You will have no paper qualifications to offer, and a reference from here would carry no weight. At forty you will not be able to pick and choose."

"There is always the kind of work that nobody else wants to do. I could train for something of that sort, grants are available."

"I see you have looked into it all very thoroughly," he said.

"Yes, I have time to think and plan. The tasks you think would madden me leave my mind free, they have that much in common with sewing mailbags."

"Nobody believes that I am capable of self-sacrifice," Jude said between clenched teeth during his four bars' silence at the start of the second variation. "I do not scream or beg for mercy, but Daniel is doing awful violence to my innermost spirit, and I shall bear it for his sake and Matthew's and my father's. If there were to be a society for the rehabilitation of Salieri, I would nominate Daniel Hardy for its first president. Now for my long G, and how long it lasts will depend on how long that bastard holds on his dotted note and what he does about the demisemiquaver. Still, I shall not reproach him : over this whole abysmal episode a decent veil shall be drawn."

"Ah, poor Daniel," Tess cried within herself, "and, oh, poor Jude! Which suffers most? The next three bars are easy and then Dan has an ascending chromatic scale, I would like to cross my fingers, but how can I and keep on playing? Tim is the colour of roast beef, underdone. His shirt is soaked through under the armpits, I suppose because of the heat, because there is nothing more to fear. It will all be over in a few minutes, the audience will clap and we shall bow and that will be that. My variation next, I shall play it very well, not to show Daniel up, only to please Tim and Daddy. Did they imagine I would not guess, putting two and two together, Tamsin so cross and sad, Mother snapping and fussing at lunchtime? I shall leave Cilrheddyn, I will train to be a nurse, Nancy will tell me how to set about it. Or I could go to a secretarial school and learn shorthand and typing; that would be better still, I should be at home to help if Mummy needs me. I know that she will need me."

"How fierce Tess looks," Daniel said, but could not allow his mind to wander, for throughout the viola variation he and Tim played gently on over her pulsing semiquavers. "When she concentrates she seems a different person, one sees her likeness to Diggory. She is not like Jude at all, he makes it look and sound so easy; nobody could doubt that Tess finds things hard and does her best with them. And I do my best, and it is not nearly good enough. But allowances will be made; that diminishes me as Jude's justifiable contempt does not. If Vincent or Matthew were to speak to me as Jude does! If I could have surprised on Matthew's face anything but a despairing goodwill, if I could strike a spark of anger off my father's slippery accommodating surface! Oh, the shame of being seen through by Dinah and her quick shrewd grasp, of being understood by Matthew, because whatever he says he can't help understanding. How deep I would go under if I were sure that every bit of me were accessible to their combined intelligences! I do not think I am so easily accessible; and in a different place where no allowances will be made that core of separate bitterness in me will expand, will drive me from thoughts and feelings into an act of living. I will write to Tess when I am fit to do so, if I am ever fit. Now she raises her head and smiles, she knows that the next bit is easier for me, Jude has four bars almost to himself. Soon it will be over, soon I shall be leaving, soon all this part of my life will be over and done with."

Meg rubbed Clare's russet hair on a towel. The little girl would not keep still, twining her arms about her mother's waist and hips, climbing with dripping feet on her mother's insteps. Harry turned away, seeing far more discomfort in this for Meg than she was aware of. "Why should I resent for her things she does not resent at all for herself?" he wondered, and then said something like it aloud.

"So long as you are not unhappy, so long as you do not feel yourself wasted."

"I am not happy all the time, who is? And there are days at a stretch sometimes when I fret and fume, but mostly I enjoy my life. I was one of a large family myself, I don't find boys and girls mysterious or alarming."

"My wife does," Harry said, with an effect of betrayal quite disproportionate to the words. "She treats our son as if he might come apart in her hands at one moment, and as if he were stuffed with high explosive the next. I take a tougher line, but the inconsistency is bad for him, we both know it."

"Shall you send him here, do you think?"

"We have decided nothing."

"Well, no, of course not, not just after a few hours. You have had no chance to talk it over."

"Yes, I meant I had decided nothing. Emma may have made up her mind, for all I know."

"Will it make any difference if she has?"

"Go and find Robert, will you?" Harry said to Clare in a voice intended to be kind, but which was roughened by the urgency of his request. Clare looked at Meg, who nodded.

"Of course it makes a difference what Emma thinks, she is my wife," he said as the child left them. "She is Robert's mother, too, I do not forget that. What were you trying to say?"

"Does she always tell you her thoughts, just as they come to her? She did not tell you about my pregnancy, there may be other things she hides."

"What are you saying?" he asked again.

"Only that to a stranger like myself it sometimes looks as if Mrs. Branksome is afraid to tell you what is in her mind."

"Why should she be afraid of me? What harm have I ever done her?"

"You will have to ask her those questions, if you want to know the answers. She may be afraid of what you could do to the child."

"What sort of a brute do you think I am?" he now cried in honest indignation.

"No sort of brute at all. I do not mean beating him or shutting him up in a cupboard, of course you would not do anything like that. But other things can take the heart out of a child."

"Women smother children, fuss over them, try to keep them babies as long as possible."

"So they do," Meg said.

"A boy has to learn a little independence of mind, if he is not to be useless."

"I expect you are right," she said, "but that is not something that can be taught; it is something that grows by itself if the conditions are favourable."

"And they are favourable here?"

"I think so, but then I am not disinterested."

"You would like my son to come here?" he said with unmistakable eagerness as she folded Clare's towel on her arm and smoothed down her damp skirt.

"Of course," she said with care, "if he would like it, and if your wife approves."

"Well, we shall see." With an effect of great daring he said, "I dare say we shall see more of you in the future, then."

"There is a Parents' Day every year," she said, "and most parents come over once or twice in the term, so, yes, we shall run into each other from time to time. And you can assure your wife that if Robert were to be homesick when he first arrives I should do everything I could for him. Boys do feel it more than girls, the first separation."

"Yes," he said, in a hollow voice of disappointment. "Yes," he repeated, taking his cue from her baffling new impersonality, "I am sure they do."

"Now they are together, they have been together for more than half an hour," Emma said. "The children are with them, of course, and I am not so stupid or so prurient as to imagine that he will be taking her in his arms and making passionate declarations of love. Harry would never do such a thing, however much he might wish to, I am as sure of that as I am that he would never steal or cheat or lie to me about anything that mattered. He is a good man labouring under a great handicap, because he has no imagination. He can feel and understand things when he has met them before; those pictures, that exhibition moved him because he has seen war and disease for himself; but if he had not they would say nothing to him. He cannot begin to think how any woman feels about her child, but he knows how a child might feel about his mother, he has a long memory. How should he understand that girl with her different experience, everything about her so different? He will think that she is frustrated and resentful; he would have been if his life had paralleled hers. He will think she will be grateful to him for taking an interest in her, when she is more likely to wish that he would leave her alone. Oh, God," Emma cried, seeing Meg's ripened beauty as clearly as if that younger woman were before her in the flesh, "let her wish that he would leave her alone."

"That pleasant fairhaired woman whose husband seems to have deserted her will burst into tears at any moment. Is it the wrong notes Daniel is playing that give her pain? I do not believe that she has heard a note of the music," Owen said. "There are my children playing their hearts out, and she is not bothering to listen. Perhaps she has a great deal on her mind and only came in here to get out of the heat. What a fool I was to forget my tablets and cause such a commotion! Though perhaps if I hadn't Daniel would not have played, thinking I would be offended, first dragged in at a moment's notice, then kicked out with equally scant ceremony. As if it matters who plays, only the music matters. Of course a fine performance is a fine thing, records are wonderful. When I have to stop work I shall listen to records a great deal. Concerts are even better, real concerts, I mean, where one can look about and see the delight in other faces and the reflection of one's own feeling makes it swell until you almost feel like shouting aloud, or weeping. Now Tess plays, and it is beautiful, it is touching, Tamsin is crying, I put my arm round her shoulders, my little love, poor child."

"Is she going to be sick like that other time?" Helen said, "or does she need to go to the lavatory? By ten she should not need to be reminded; I didn't remind her, I was with Owen, and of course Diggory would not have thought of it. But the music is nearly over, I will smile at her encouragingly, so she will know there is not much longer to wait. The years and years and years it takes for a child to grow, and yet sometimes it seems all to have gone in a flash, and I can hardly believe they were ever babies lying in their prams and crying, crying. How they cried, Jude especially; now he is putting those lungs to better use. And oh, it is cruel that I cannot enjoy his work or feel any proper pride in what he is doing because of this awful thing that we have to face now, and that I swear we don't deserve. What have we ever done, Owen of all people, who never hurt a fly, what have we done to be punished so horribly? Wicked, greedy, criminal people grow old and have nothing to worry about; their cars and houses and clothes are all paid for without a day's skimping or saving. And Owen is not even to see his children grow up and marry." She shook her head to bring herself back into the real world. "Still, they are lovely children, all of them; I wouldn't have had a different life myself even if it had been possible. I don't believe Owen would have wanted any other life, only more of this one." She drove away that thought too with resolution. "It is kind of Dinah Hardy to offer to drive us home. She can sleep in Jude's room, his mattress is the best. But Tess has flowered curtains and a carpet; and the books in there would be more suitable. I shall put Tamsin and Owen to bed the moment we get home, then Dinah and I can sit in the garden and talk. Or she can talk, and I will listen. She is so amusing and lively, she will cheer me up. I expect I shall feel a little low tonight, it will have been such a long day, and so hot, so hot."

"It was your fault," Robert said. "It was your idea."

"You wanted him. You asked to keep him. This morning he was running about as happy as could be whisking his little tail. And now he is all stiff and dead, and it is your fault, not mine."

Meg and Harry came up in time to hear the end of this colloquy: the children stood by the open boot of Harry's car, an empty box in Robert's hand, the corpse of a mouse in Clare's.

"Did you shut that little creature up in a box with no water?" Harry said, looking at his son with more disgust than anger. "You should have known better. You are not a baby."

"How should he know?" Clare said, ranging herself on Robert's side by some fantastic operation of sex and size and common fear of Harry's voice. "He never had a pet before, and now he has lost this one. I ought to have remembered about the water."

"Yes, and another time you will remember," Meg said, taking the dead thing from her daughter and putting it back into the box that had been its death-chamber and might as well now serve as a coffin. "We will bury him with the others."

"Have some of the others died?" Robert asked Clare, snatching a crumb of comfort from the knowledge that the deaths of other mice could not be visited on him.

"Yes, they are always doing it. Otherwise there would be more mice in the world than anything else because they have babies all the time they are alive."

"If I did decide to come here," Robert said, keeping his eyes off his father, "would you sell me two mice and show me how to look after them?"

"I might."

"You would give him some, Clare, wouldn't you?" Meg said.

"I would rather sell them. I should have some more money to put in my box and he would take better care of the mice. Diggory says people only value the things they pay for."

"Bravo, Diggory," Harry said. "Go and get some clothes on, Robert. The concert is nearly over. As soon as Mummy has said goodbye to Miss Storace we must be on our way."

"You, too, Clare. You must not catch cold, the end of term is a busy time for me. I cannot do with nursing you too."

When the children had gone Harry took Meg's hand. She made no resistance : there was nobody to see them in the court-yard but it would have made no difference if there had been, even if Emma herself were a witness. His grasp was an apology for some things misapprehended, a hint of truer understanding to come; when they moved apart he relinquished all those intentions he could not have formulated even in his innermost thoughts, and she saw what those intentions must have been and wondered over them before she dismissed them for ever. The obstinate beautiful girl he had remembered he now laid to rest like an exorcised ghost; and how should it hurt her to know she had been often in his thoughts when for this one day at least she had found it hard to keep him out of her own?

"Janet has chosen funereal flowers for the fireplace," Matthew said. "She must have had Daniel in mind and his chimney sweep. I can see lilies, white gladiolus and phlox with darkest glossy leaves, almost black. The only colour is in the centres of the marguerites and they are almost as bright as Kate's hair is now, with specks of golden dust in the shaft of sunlight that plays over her head; when that hair fades she will be as clever as her mother at finding ways to bring back its glory. What will become

of all t.. beauty and obstinacy, the pathos of her self regard?
They endlessly regard themselves, these children, turning about
to surprise each other in new attitudes, trying on ideas and
experiences, as if they were free to choose what to discard, never
guessing what is done is usually done for ever. But now I must
attend, for the tempo is changing; here is the fifth variation,
ushered in by modulations that shock even me at the hundredth
hearing. For that commonplace little tune is about to be trans-
formed, a miracle is to be worked upon it, and before we are
allowed to hear it again in all its ordinary prettiness it will be
shown to us dressed for heaven, an intimation, a promise, the
Word of God."